GRANNY GETS GHOSTED

A SECRET AGENT GRANNY MYSTERY BOOK 12

HARPER LIN

This is a work of fiction. Names, characters, organizations, places, events, and incidents are either products of the author's imagination or are used fictitiously.

GRANNY GETS GHOSTED

ISBN: 978-1-997777-01-4

www.harperlin.com

ONE

If there was one thing Cheerville was good at, it was turning the mundane into an event. The annual rummage sale became the "Antique Extravaganza." A bake sale that raised twenty dollars was called a "culinary fundraiser." If someone so much as trimmed a hedge into the vague shape of an animal, the town newsletter called it an "art installation." We couldn't even host a pancake breakfast without calling it the "Maple Syrup Jubilee." And don't even get me started on the Christmas tree lighting. It had been rebranded three times in five years, each version arriving with a new logo and a new committee. The latest slogan promised "unity through sparkle." None of them managed to fix the same old string of lights that never worked on the first try.

For an ordinary town, this town seemed to live in perpetual fear of being ordinary. Someone was always ready to weaponize a holiday by forming a subcommittee or printing matching T-shirts. You could sneeze downtown and someone would make it part of an annual "Health Awareness Fair." People here needed a reason to gather every other week, and if one didn't exist, they made it up, complete with raffle tickets and refreshments.

Halloween was when the Historical Society truly came alive. October gave them purpose. They came out of their offices armed with clipboards, ready to transform every half-forgotten alley and abandoned barn into something "historic." Costumes were debated like policy, props were treated like relics, and flyers featured creative writing that would make actual historians cry.

It kept everyone busy, I suppose. By mid-month, you couldn't buy black fabric anywhere in town, and the craft store owner developed a haunted look of her own. The Historical Society moved through the streets like an occupying force with glue guns. They had matching tote bags, color-coded schedules, and a frightening amount of enthusiasm. Even the mayor stayed out of their way after last year's "Pumpkin Incident," which involved an argument between two volunteers over artistic integrity, and a trip to urgent care.

This year, they decided to prove that this town was steeped in legend. After months of committee meetings that included coffee and arguments over fonts, they announced the grand project that would outshine every parade and cemetery tour that came before it: the first-ever Cheerville Ghost Walk. It was marketed as "an immersive historical experience" in bold, gothic type.

The idea was simple enough: a guided nighttime stroll through our "dark past." It was a mix of history, performance, and whatever passed for spookiness in a town where the scariest thing that usually happened was a squirrel getting into the attic. The Society promised "immersive storytelling." Pamphlets promised "unforgettable chills." And the local paper devoted three full columns to it, along with an artist's sketch of a ghost floating tastefully over the town square.

This town certainly had its shadows, with murders, mobsters, and scandals that never quite died, but we weren't known for the supernatural. Still, that never stopped anyone here. We had never let the truth get in the way of a good brochure.

The Widow was the only good ghost story

Cheerville could claim. In some versions her husband was a wealthy merchant. In others he was a riverboat captain or a bootlegger who disappeared during Prohibition. One tale had him dragged into the tunnels under town. Another insisted he had been tossed into the river by smugglers. Whatever the details, the ending was always the same. The Widow dressed in black, crying into a handkerchief, waiting forever for a coffin that never arrived.

The town's older residents swore she had once lived in the grand white house on Whitcomb Hill on the edge of town, though no one could quite agree which one that was. There were at least three houses that claimed the title, all conveniently available for short-term rentals during October.

If you lived here long enough, you'd hear all the minute details from locals' mouths. Romantic types said the Widow died of heartbreak. Pragmatists blamed pneumonia. Teenagers claimed she cursed anyone who didn't believe she existed. Skeptics just agreed she made a good excuse to sell souvenirs and flashlight batteries. Every year, someone claimed to have recorded her weeping on their phone, only for it to turn out to be wind, frogs, or a badly tuned radio. That never stopped the next person from trying.

For the Society's purposes, ghost stories weren't

about accuracy but atmosphere. Change the husband's line of work, add smugglers, remove smugglers, it made no difference as long as the audience leaned in to listen. Tourists were not paying for a history lesson. They were paying for a chill down the spine and a paper cup of cocoa. During fall in Cheerville, cocoa sales were the true measure of success. The Historical Society's treasurer had the numbers to prove it.

So the Ghost Walk became a mix of the town's genuine history, which included bootlegging and plenty of real crime, wrapped in the gauze of the Widow's legend. The town's past was dark enough without ghosts, but a little smoke and a few mournful sobs from a volunteer in costume made it more profitable. If you offered a bit of atmosphere and a souvenir mug, people would line up around the block. When ticket sales opened, the Society was already congratulating itself. They sold out every ticket and declared the whole thing "historic."

A committee had been meeting for six months, and they treated the planning like it was the United Nations. Every decision was recorded in minutes typed neatly and printed out for the record, as if anyone would ever read them again, especially since every meeting ended in squabbles that lasted longer than the agenda itself. They argued over font sizes as if the fate of Cheerville depended on whether "Gothic" or "Caslon" carried more mystery. They spent a full evening debating the cocoa, with one camp insisting it had to be organic and another insisting nobody in town could tell the difference.

By the fourth meeting, I heard one woman threaten to resign over a dispute about streamer placements. Another cried when her mural proposal got cut for budget reasons. I wasn't even on the committee, and yet by the time I heard the gossip, I needed a drink.

The Historical Society finally declared victory when they agreed on paper cups. Each one bore the Widow in silhouette, her veil trailing down the side like a stamp of approval from the grave. They all congratulated themselves on this marketing genius.

So for one week in October, lanterns, cobwebs, and a few well-timed shrieks let them pretend our little town had secrets as chilling as Salem's.

And then there was me.

I should know better. I have survived coups, bombings, and more than one double-cross in my life. I have been double-crossed, shot at, and nearly blown up on three different continents. Yet somehow, here I was in a creaky nineteenth-century carriage house, volunteering to check the placement of fake cobwebs and making sure the mannequins didn't topple over.

That was retirement for you.

I'm Barbara Gold. Age: 71. Eyes: blue. Hair: gray. Weight: still classified. Skills: undercover surveillance, firearms, and the ability to look like a harmless granny while considering fifty ways to kill you with a knitting needle. Current status: retired widow and grandmother, trying to keep a low profile in a town where the loudest scandal last month was a bake sale that ran out of pies too early.

Addendum to current status: inspecting "haunted" décor for the Historical Society's inaugural Halloween Ghost Walk.

I didn't even plan on being here tonight. Liz had been the one who signed up as a volunteer, insisting that she needed something "to do with her hands" since early retirement had left her restless. I promised her an hour. Liz had never directly stated what she used to do before she retired, but I'd seen her neutralize a man with a flick of her wrist, and she hadn't learned that in yoga class. She'd dropped enough hints, and my best guess was something covert, maybe Black Ops. She likely went on assignments the government never put on paper. Whatever it was, she knew enough to have strong suspicions about me.

Housewifery didn't really suit her, the way retirement didn't suit me. If she wasn't scrubbing baseboards with military precision, she was rearranging her pantry for the third time in a week or pacing the kitchen like a soldier waiting for deployment. The Ghost Walk was the first community project that managed to hold her attention for longer than an afternoon, and she had pounced on it as if someone had handed her a mission briefing with **TOP SECRET** stamped across the top.

Liz threw herself into it with the kind of seriousness most people reserved for tax audits. By the second meeting, the Historical Society had learned not to argue with her. They nodded politely and let her take charge of the lighting plan, the sound cues, and the proper way to drape cheesecloth so that it suggested decay instead of a messy tablecloth.

I sometimes wondered if she missed command chains. If the Ghost Walk had given her the closest thing to a mission she'd had in years, that was a good thing. And since I have an appalling weakness for loyalty, I let her drag me into it.

"Come on, Barbara, it will be fun," she had said with a perfectly straight face.

I agreed to come along for the final inspection.

Now here we were, standing in the drafty carriage house, faux lanterns swinging on iron hooks, the whole place decked out with just enough spooky décor to fool the tourists. The lantern light certainly gave it atmosphere. Shadows pooled in corners, and mannequins seemed to breathe when the wind rattled the windows.

"Gotta hand it to them," Liz said, scanning the room like she was assessing a threat perimeter instead of papier-mâché. "For a small-town production, this is solid work."

Liz did not hand out compliments lightly, which was enough to make me look again.

"Especially the Widow," I agreed, nodding toward the mannequin in black.

The figure was bent over a coffin, veil spilling forward to hide her painted face. Her gloved hands were frozen in mid-reach, caught forever in a gesture of loss. A lantern had been positioned to stretch her shadow across the floorboards, so that she seemed to hover rather than stand. From a distance, she almost looked real. Up close, the illusion cracked. The veil was polyester, the gloves were costume-store satin, and the faint smell of paint still clung to her like bad perfume. But the longer you looked, the harder it was to shake the feeling that something might look back.

Since the Ghost Walk brochures had been distributed, there had been more whispers about her. Some swore they had seen a veil drifting through the churchyard, brushing against the gravestones. Others claimed they had heard a woman's sobs carried on the wind, always in the middle of the night. The Historical Society leaned hard on those stories. They promised that if visitors lingered in the carriage house after dark, they might hear the Widow's weeping for themselves.

The brochures called her "Cheerville's Most Enduring Mystery." Someone had even made collectible pins of her silhouette, which meant that by next week, every fourth-grader in town would have one pinned to their backpack.

I turned back to Liz, expecting her usual eye-roll at such nonsense. Instead, she was still staring at the mannequin in black, her head tilted slightly, as if listening for something. That made me pause.

"You don't actually think this place is haunted," I said, half teasing and half incredulous.

Her mouth curved just enough to pass for a smirk. "I think it's entertaining."

I was ready to nod and move on, but then she added, "But yes. Maybe I do. At least a little."

I blinked. Liz, of all people? "You? Believing in ghosts?"

She shrugged, the movement casual. "I've seen things on deployments I can't explain. Once, in Kandahar, my unit swore we heard footsteps circling our perimeter in the dead of night. We didn't see any footprints. No animals either. We just heard the sound of boots crunching the dirt. It happened three nights in a row. Even the sergeant, who mocked anyone who carried a good luck charm, refused to stand watch alone after that."

I snorted. "And you think that means ghosts?"

Liz's smile was faint. "It means I keep an open mind. Not everything leaves evidence you can file in a report."

"Or," I said, "it means someone was sneaking around who was very good at covering their tracks. Which, if you ask me, is far more frightening than a ghost."

Her laugh was low and genuine. "Always the skeptic."

"Always the realist," I said.

A shackled skeleton slumped in front of a rough wooden alcove, its plastic arms chained to the "entrance" as though it had died guarding the secret. Above it, a hand-painted sign in shaky lettering declared: The Smuggler's Cell.

It was supposed to be the big draw of the Ghost Walk, their pièce de résistance. This was one of the Historical Society's proudest set pieces. They had built the alcove themselves, nailing together rough planks and pushing it flush against the far wall of the carriage house. They'd hauled in crates stamped with fake shipping marks and stacked them to the side of the alcove.

The idea was that it represented the hidden entrance to the legendary tunnels under Cheerville, the ones locals had gossiped about for years but that no one had ever actually proven to exist. The tunnels were the kind of story that showed up in every small town, whispered about by teenagers who swore they had a friend who had a cousin who had seen them. No one had ever produced evidence. That had not stopped the Society from trying to make the tale look real. Every member of the committee had taken turns admiring their handiwork, convinced it was museum-worthy.

It was meant to look ominous, and at a distance it did. The boards were uneven, painted in streaks of brown and black to imitate rot. The hinges were coated with reddish paint to mimic rust. In the dim lantern light, the illusion worked well enough. A tourist could easily imagine a hidden passage stretching out under the town. But up close, it was less convincing. The entire panel sagged against the frame, the top right corner noticeably lower than the rest, as if the fake door was exhausted from the effort of standing upright.

Liz noticed the flaw. Her eyes narrowed as she studied the angle. "That door's crooked," she muttered.

I gave it a glance and shrugged. "So? It's a Halloween prop. Crooked gives it character."

"Not that kind of crooked." She crouched, inspecting the frame with calm detachment. "I helped build this alcove last week. We lined it up straight. We made sure the panels sat flush against the wall. The door was even then."

That caught my attention. Before I could reply, she reached for the skeleton. The chains jingled as she shifted it aside. The plastic bones clattered together like wind chimes. The skeleton sagged in her hands as Liz propped it against the wall.

"Sorry, pal," she said to the skeleton, "we'll put you back later."

Once it was moved, she pressed one hand against

the planks, meaning only to push the door back into line. Instead, the entire panel gave way. It fell under her touch with a sudden jolt, hinges and all, as though it had never been nailed securely.

The sound split the air. Liz stumbled back a half step.

Then it happened quickly.

From the hollow space behind it, a figure lurched forward, brushing past the skeleton and pitching toward me.

I didn't try to catch him. Instinct told me better. Years of training had drilled into me that letting a falling body drag you down was an easy way to end up injured or worse. Instead, I shifted my weight just enough to the side and allowed gravity to do its work. He crumpled to the floorboards at my feet with a heavy, ungraceful thud. Dust puffed up from the floor.

I had seen plenty of bodies fall before. You never forgot the sound. The lantern beside me swung slightly on its hook, throwing light in a sharp arc across the room. For a moment the shadows danced along the wall, then steadied, and the beam landed squarely across his face.

It was a man. Mid-fifties, perhaps. His skin was pale in a way that had nothing to do with lantern light. His jaw hung slack, and his head lolled at an angle that no healthy person could manage. One glance told me this was no fainting spell.

My eyes tracked the details, cataloguing them out of habit. There was no tension left in his jaw, no fight in his muscles. Whatever fear or pain he had felt was long past. But rope burns circled his wrists, raw and red against the pale skin. They looked recent, marks that came from being tied tight for a long stretch of time. His suit had once been pressed and neat, but now it was a ruin, the fabric streaked with dust and dirt. There were scuffs at the knees, a tear at one elbow, all the signs of someone who had not walked here under his own power. His shoes caught my attention next, expensive-looking polished black leather. A smear of mud clung to one heel. He had been somewhere damp before he ended up here.

The picture was clear. He had been dragged. Dragged and then shoved into that false alcove like a piece of unwanted luggage, hidden behind the stage prop for someone to find, eventually.

Liz dropped down beside him in an instant. Her movements were quick but not panicked. She leaned over him, scanning his face, his posture, the marks on his wrists. Her expression remained neutral, her mind working behind the mask. For those few seconds she was all calculation, a professional slipping back into the habits of old work.

Then I saw the change. The cool, detached look gave way to recognition.

"Patrick," she said at last.

The name meant little to me, but it clearly meant something to her.

TWO

"Who is he?" I asked.

Liz didn't answer right away. She was still in that mode of hers, the one that made her useful in any crisis and unbearable at a dinner table. She catalogued everything. Her mind worked like a filing cabinet with names, dates, and gestures, all slotted into their proper place. She looked at the scene the way a surveyor looks at land, measuring angles no one else could see.

She moved her head, taking in the details. She squinted at every particle of dust. The dust on his shoes, the scuffs on the floor, the position of his hands. She was already reconstructing the last few minutes of his life.

Her lips moved. She was speaking to herself,

running silent calculations. Somewhere behind her eyes, a map was forming, the route from life to death traced in quiet precision.

"This doesn't make sense," she said finally, almost to herself. "He was fine just a few days ago. I remember him."

I crouched beside her, more to watch her reaction than to look at Patrick. The lantern light cut across her face. She looked stern but not frightened. Shock registered in her differently. It turned to focus instead of fear. She didn't waste emotion until she knew where to put it. I respected that.

"You don't think this was an accident," I said.

Her gaze lifted to mine. "No," she said flatly. "This was deliberate."

"Who is he?" I asked again, more firmly this time. "You said you knew him?"

She nodded once. "Patrick Halloway. He was on the committee for the Ghost Walk. That's how I know him. We all saw him at the last meeting. He was the one who wanted to move the lantern stand closer to the gate."

I didn't know him. I waited, expecting more, but Liz didn't offer it. Her eyes had already gone back to Patrick, studying his posture, the angle of his arm, the way one leg bent too sharply at the knee.

"That's it?" I pressed. "What did he do for work?"

"Something with antiques," she said.

"Antiques dealer?"

"I think so." Her tone turned thoughtful. "I remember him talking to anyone who would listen during a coffee break about a shipment he was expecting. I never visited his shop, but he seemed very passionate about antiques. He was excited about a Victorian writing desk, and some old Civil War letters. There were other things, but I don't remember."

"Doesn't sound like the kind of thing that gets a man killed," I said. "But still, an antique dealer. Talking about treasures one week, and the next..."

I didn't bother finishing. His body said the rest.

It was hard to tell under the lantern light, but my guess was that he had been dead less than a day. The rope burns suggested he was tied up first. Perhaps the killer or killers didn't know what to do with him at first, before deciding he needed to be silenced for good.

A draft slid across the floor, and the fake cobwebs shivered in its path. For a second, they looked alive. The movement was small but unsettling.

Liz straightened slowly, one hand braced on her

knee. The other hovered near her hip, fingers twitching as though they wanted something to hold. She turned away from Patrick, blinking rapidly. The distance between recognition and comprehension had just closed for her. In her mind, the man who had smiled across a committee table, talking about lantern placement and ticket sales, had turned into the body cooling on the floorboards. I knew the look. It was the moment you stopped seeing a person and started seeing them as evidence. Caring too soon blurred the edges of what mattered.

"We need to call it in," I said finally. "I'll do it."

Liz gave a single, sober nod. "Right."

I stayed crouched a moment longer. Before standing, I nodded toward his wrists. "Did you notice that?"

The skin around them was marked in raw rings, angry red against the pale flesh.

Liz's mouth pressed thin. "Someone tied him up first," she said. "Then dragged him in here and dumped him in the alcove."

The words had no hesitation. She had seen enough restraint injuries in her time to know what they meant. Her certainty left no room for doubt. I rose beside her, dusting my palms against my trousers.

I looked at the body again.

"But why?" I asked.

Liz didn't answer.

Then the skeleton's chains stirred in the draft, a faint rattle that sounded as if it were trying to get our attention. The props, for all their dust and artifice, seemed to whisper their own story. Patrick, however, remained silent. This place certainly had a sense of irony.

I slipped a hand into my pocket, fingers closing around the coolness of my phone, then pulled it out.

THE GLOW of headlights cut across the yard, washing the windows in harsh white before the red and blue lights followed. They flashed in rhythm, throwing stripes of color across the walls. The props looked almost cheerful under police lights. Cheerville couldn't sleep through a siren. I expected half the town to be outside soon.

Chief Grimal never sent his officers in first if he could help it. He liked to make his grand entrance alone. Sure enough, the door swung open with a heavy thud, and there he was, broad frame filling the threshold. He narrowed his eyes at the sight of us, not bothering to greet us.

His flashlight beam cut through the space like he was slicing it open. Two uniforms followed close at his back, boots heavy on the floor. A third officer trailed behind, already flipping open a notepad before he even looked at the body.

"Well," Grimal said in a voice too loud for the room, "what've we got?"

The light paused over the skeleton, then drifted to the coffin prop, then caught the still figure on the floor. His shoulders stiffened for a second before he covered it with a grunt.

Liz and I stepped back automatically, giving him space to loom.

"We found him," I said. "He was hidden in the fake alcove."

Grimal's flashlight wavered slightly as he crouched. His knees cracked loud enough to make one of the younger officers suppress a smile. He studied Patrick for a long, quiet moment. Then he jerked his chin toward his men, the way a man calls a dog to heel.

"Mark the scene," he said. "No one touches anything until the coroner's here. And clear the yard.

Every citizen in town is probably already making their way here."

One officer gave a brisk nod and hurried out. His radio crackled to life, spitting static and half-formed words. Through the open door, I could see the glow of cell phone screens rising as townspeople filmed the commotion. Cheerville didn't need reporters with an audience this built-in.

Grimal straightened slowly, brushing his palms against his thighs. His eyes landed on Liz and me. "You two again," he said. "I should start charging rent for all the crime scenes you show up to."

I smiled, all warmth and no apology. "We're volunteers, Chief. Just checking the decorations."

Liz stood beside me, silent and watching him with a look that could file metal. He caught it but didn't comment. That was one thing I respected about him. He knew when to quit while he was behind.

Grimal's flashlight swung again. The beam landed on the coffin prop, then on the Widow mannequin. His lip curled, disdain tightening his whole face. "Is this nonsense supposed to be part of a haunted house?"

"It's for the Historical Society's Ghost Walk," I

reminded him. My tone stayed pleasant. That only irritated him more.

"Hmph." He tugged at his belt. "Now I've got a body dumped right in the middle of it. Perfect."

One of the younger officers made the mistake of letting out a nervous laugh. Grimal turned on him with a glare that could have frozen water.

"Focus," Grimal barked. "Get that crowd back before they start sneaking in here for souvenirs."

The officer stumbled over a "yes, sir" and bolted for the door.

When Grimal turned back to us, the anger had drained into something colder. "Stay put till I get your statements," he said. "No wandering. No disappearing before I'm done, you hear?"

"Yes, sir," I said, in mock politeness.

Grimal's eyes narrowed again, but he didn't bother replying. He turned his light away, sweeping it one more time across the props. The Widow's veil stirred just then, lifted by a stray current of air. The lace shifted as if something beneath it had taken a breath.

Grimal froze for a fraction of a second. I saw the small, involuntary tightening of his mouth before he caught himself. He twitched, then muttered something under his breath while stalking off. For a man who didn't believe in ghosts, he certainly looked like he'd just met one.

THREE

By the time I made it home, the night chill still clung to me like a lingering cold. The damp air was a reminder that autumn was nearly halfway to winter. Still, I drove with the window cracked open to smell the wet leaves and to wash the musty smell of the carriage house off of me.

I had taken Liz back to her house first. She could have walked her driveway with her eyes shut and not missed a step. She didn't need me there, and we both knew it, but after finding someone she knew dead at the carriage house, it seemed the decent thing to do. Even soldiers need an escort once in a while.

She didn't talk during the drive. She was the kind of person who only spoke when she had the words ready. When I pulled into her driveway, she thanked me the way Liz thanked anyone. A nod, a word, and then she squared her shoulders and disappeared inside. That was her way of saying she was fine. Whether or not she was, I let her keep that story.

The drive to my own house was quiet. Most of Cheerville was asleep, or pretended to be. But quiet didn't mean ignorance, not when sirens cut the night. Half the town would have heard them, and by morning everyone would know there had been a dead body of a local found at the carriage house. By noon they would be debating whether it tied back to the Widow. By supper there would be three competing versions, none of them true, but each told with confidence.

I pulled into my driveway already hearing those stories in my head. Inside, I hung up my jacket. The kitchen light was too bright after hours of lantern glow. I dimmed it, the bulb humming faintly as it settled. I put the kettle on out of habit. I brewed a cup of tea I had no intention of finishing, but a teacup on the table made the kitchen feel normal, even if nothing about the night had been. The creak of the odd floorboard reminded me of being at the carriage house.

The carriage house was taped off now, police

cars stationed there, officers on guard. Patrick's body belonged to them for the time being. It was their problem for now. That was fine by me.

What I had seen told me enough. Patrick Halloway's death was not an accident. The "why" wasn't obvious, but I was not in the habit of leaving questions unanswered.

What I remembered of the scene wouldn't let go. The rope burns, the fresh drag marks, the way the body was simply dumped and left in the fake alcove. Just in time for Halloween, too. What did I need to do to hear the ending of this disturbing tale?

My cat Dandelion appeared without a sound, gliding into the kitchen. He leapt onto the chair beside me and began grooming one paw. His yellow eyes flicked up at me once, unimpressed.

"I know," I said. "You'd prefer I stick to crocheting."

He gave a low, disapproving chirp and resumed cleaning. That was Dandelion's version of moral support: quiet judgment. He had the expression of an old philosopher. Sometimes I thought he understood more than he should.

I sat at the table, set the teacup down, and opened my laptop. I started typing.

Patrick Halloway Cheerville Antiques

The screen glowed in the dim kitchen, reflecting faintly off Dandelion's fur. He stopped licking long enough to peer at the light, then blinked once as if unimpressed by my persistence and curled himself into a loaf beside me.

The shop's homepage loaded first. It wasn't modern or flashy, but professional enough. Patrick's face sat squarely in the center of it, smiling stiffly in a tailored suit.

The background looked staged: an old desk that was probably dusted five minutes before the photo, a stack of leather-bound books that no one had ever opened, and a vase of flowers doing its best to pretend the place didn't smell faintly of mothballs. Someone had told Patrick to look "approachable," and he had obeyed with the enthusiasm of a man posing for a passport photo.

The man in that photograph looked very much alive. The man I had seen fall out from behind a false door hours earlier did not resemble him at all. That was the trick with death. It stripped away the varnish, and left you with whatever remained underneath.

I clicked through the product pages. Each one opened to more of the same, items you would expect to find in a small-town antiques store, curated to look rarer than they really were. Victorian armchairs sagging in the middle. Worn velvet cushions. Silver-plated serving sets polished to a dull shine, gleaming but not valuable. Oil portraits of stern ancestors, whose descendants must've decided they would rather look at blank walls.

He sold nostalgia to people who wanted to feel cultured without leaving Cheerville. His customers wanted pieces that were conversation starters. All of it respectable enough, but nothing that explained why Patrick had ended up dead.

I checked the Google reviews next. Rows of them scrolled down the screen, each one short and mostly positive.

"Knowledgeable dealer."

"A bit overpriced, but worth it for rare finds."

"Imported pieces you will not see anywhere else."

Sometimes customers bragged about their purchases with pride. A clock from Vienna. Brass lanterns from India. A sofa from Scotland.

I checked the dates. The most recent review had been posted just three days ago. The customer gushed about a set of "early European navigational tools," praising Patrick's uncanny ability to track down what no one else could find.

The phrasing caught my attention. "Uncanny ability." Did he discover something he shouldn't have, or something so valuable that someone needed to kill for it?

Dandelion had fallen asleep beside me, tail curled like a comma. I envied his ability to rest anywhere.

I went back to the website homepage, staring at Patrick's stiff smile. I didn't know how much time passed before I heard a knock at my front door.

It wasn't a tentative knock or an urgent one, but gentle and familiar. I closed the laptop and pushed my chair back. Octavian. He had mentioned swinging by tonight. In all the chaos, I'd forgotten.

I glanced at the clock on the wall. It was earlier than I thought. I rubbed my eyes once, pushing away the fatigue that came from thinking too much.

Crossing the living room, I carried on a recent internal debate when it came to him. Should I give him a key? It wasn't the first time the thought had surfaced. It made sense. We were long past the stage of dating. He had settled into my life with an ease I had once thought impossible. He knew my kitchen better than I did. He knew which drawer held the wooden spoons, which cupboard held the teas, which pan I favored for eggs. He had cooked here often enough that the place felt like his as much as mine. A key would only make things easier.

But old habits clung hard. Keys meant access. Access meant risk. I had memorized too many exit routes, carried too many aliases, and changed too many locks to hand someone that kind of trust without hesitation.

Octavian was not a threat, not in any way my rational mind could argue. Yet another part of me, the part that never truly rested even in the safest bed, bristled at the idea of anyone being able to cross my threshold without my permission. I had built a life on control. Handing over a key felt like letting go of safety.

Besides, Octavian had a trusting streak that made me nervous. He often left his car unlocked in his own driveway, and once lent his lawnmower to a neighbor who never gave it back. It was charming in a maddening sort of way. I suspected that if I gave him a key, he'd make a spare "just in case" and who knew where he would misplace it. He was a good man, but a terrible custodian of small objects.

The knock came again. I opened the door.

There he was, framed by the porch light. His smile was already waiting for me. He had a grocery bag in one hand, balanced against his hip as if it weighed nothing. The sight of him was disarming. He always had that effect on me.

"Hungry yet?" he asked, lifting the bag slightly.

"Always," I replied, stepping aside to let him in.

He walked past me with the quiet confidence of a man who knew exactly where he was going. He set the bag on the counter and began unpacking with the same efficiency he brought to everything. Out came pasta, bread, cheese, eggs, and a bottle of wine. Nothing fancy, but I knew he would whip this into something that would taste like it belonged in a restaurant.

Dandelion, who was woken up by the sound of his entry, hopped onto a nearby stool, sniffed the grocery bag once, decided eggs were beneath him, and settled in to supervise with a slow blink.

"You're spoiling me," I said to Octavian, leaning against the counter.

"Hardly." He rinsed his hands at the sink, sleeves pushed up. He dried them on the striped towel I kept on the oven handle without looking.

I had spent my life working with people who thrived on tension. Octavian was the opposite of that. It brought me a comfort I'd never known before.

I watched him as he filled a pot and set it to boil as if it were the most fascinating thing in the world.

There was something about the sight of him in my kitchen. He belonged here, in my home, in my life. This had once been my space alone. Now he made it look as though it had always been ours. He kept olive oil on the counter now, a pepper mill near the stove, and a spare corkscrew in the drawer I used to reserve for batteries. He had left a toothbrush in the medicine cabinet last week. I had pushed it to the side, then centered it again.

The thought circled again, the one that had needled me on the way to the door. Should I give him a key? The answer turned over and over inside me like a coin tossed and never caught.

I reached for the wine, pouring two glasses. I handed him one, and for a moment I let the small domesticity of the scene hold me still. The clink of glass against glass, the weight of company at my counter, the smell of bread waiting to be sliced. It was almost enough to make me forget myself, convincing me that danger lived somewhere else.

Remembering my manners, I tilted my glass and asked, "So, how was your day?"

He gave me a half-amused look over the rim of his glass. "I was at the Historical Society with Tyler."

"Right, I forgot. Your first training session."

"Yes," Octavian said. He sipped his wine before

adding, "The boy's enthusiastic, I'll give him that. Tyler has more facts in his head than most professors I've met, and he's not shy about unloading them on anyone willing to listen." He chuckled, shaking his head. "At one point, he started quoting municipal bylaws about excavation rights. I think the others were ready to fake fainting to make him stop."

I smirked. "Sounds like someone else I know."

He gave me a sidelong glance but ignored the jab. Instead, he went on. "He has a real passion for Cheerville's history. Especially the Prohibition years. He recited dates, names, even descriptions of old shipping manifests. You'd think he had lived through it the way he told it."

Tyler was the Historical Society's golden boy, bright, eager, always ready to volunteer. They had put him in charge of training tour guides for the Ghost Walk, which explained why Octavian had sat through lectures about smuggling routes and grain taxes.

"So you'll definitely be a tour guide," I said.

Octavian nodded and took another sip of his wine. "It'll be fun. Tyler was delighted to have an audience who actually knew what he was talking about. I think he believes the ghost stories too."

"Does he?" I raised an eyebrow. "And you?"

Octavian swirled his wine before answering. "I told him stories like that make the Ghost Walk more exciting. Hidden passageways, secret doors, ghostly figures drifting through the churchyard. It gives people something to imagine."

I tilted my head. "So you encouraged him?"

"I didn't discourage him," Octavian said with a small shrug. "He's young. Let him believe in mysteries under the town."

I let out a quiet hum, neither agreeing nor disagreeing. I had seen enough mysteries in my time, and I knew most of them turned shabby when the facts were dragged into daylight. Ghosts were no exception. If Tyler wanted to put his faith in sobbing widows and phantom footsteps, that was his business.

Octavian caught my expression and smiled. "Tyler would be crushed if he saw you looking that skeptical."

"I wasn't looking skeptical," I said evenly, though the corners of my mouth tugged downward in spite of me.

"Mm." His smile widened. "Maybe not. But I told him if anyone in town could dig up the truth about its ghosts, it would be you."

I gave him a flat look. "You told him that?"

"I did." His grin stayed in place, unbothered. "You've got a reputation, Barbara. People notice when you're around. He'll be waiting for you to prove him right."

"Then he'll be waiting a long time," I said, taking another sip of wine, letting the taste settle sharp against my tongue. Too many people in this town knew who I was. The less people noticed, the easier it was to move quietly.

Octavian leaned against the counter, glass loose in his hand, the picture of ease. His smile softened, almost teasing. "So, what did you get up to while I was memorizing ghost stories and family legends? Don't tell me you were off solving another mystery without me."

I arched an eyebrow, keeping my voice calm. "Not quite." I let the pause stretch, long enough that his easy smile began to waver. Then I said casually, "I did find a body, though."

That wiped the amusement clean off his face. The wine glass almost slipped and he tightened his fingers around the glass.

"A body?"

I nodded once, letting him see that I was not joking. "At the carriage house."

He stared at me for a heartbeat, trying to decide

if this was one of my dry jokes. When I didn't crack a smile, he set the glass down carefully, as though he suddenly needed both hands free. His eyes narrowed, reading my face. "You're serious."

"As serious as it gets. You didn't see the police cars?"

"I didn't drive past the carriage house." Octavian exhaled slowly. "Who..."

"Patrick Halloway," I said. "Sells antiques at—"

"I know him!" he exclaimed. "What happened to him?"

"That's what I'm trying to figure out," I said.

I gave him the outline of the discovery with Liz, but I kept the story neat without any of the gruesome details. If Octavian knew Patrick, he didn't need those images lodged in his head. Protecting someone wasn't always about keeping them safe. Sometimes it was about keeping them comfortable.

Octavian listened, his frown deepening. "But he was kind. He sold me my clock just last month, the brass one in my study. He spent twenty minutes telling me about its mechanism, how it was once kept in a merchant's parlor. That man talked to me for ages about the history of that clock. He told me how to wind it, how to keep it running another hundred years if I cared to. He had such a passion for antiques. He loved what he did." He shook his head slowly. "He even wrapped the thing in so much newspaper I thought I'd bought a mummy."

"He sounds like he paid attention to detail," I muttered. I shook my head too. "It's a shame."

Octavian leaned back against the kitchen sink. "Are you sure it wasn't an accident? Maybe he wandered into that alcove and had a heart attack? It happens. People collapse all the time. Perhaps that's all it was."

"I don't think so, darling." The words left my mouth quiet but certain. The evidence had already ruled that out.

He looked troubled. If he had been there, he would have tried CPR or called an ambulance. The thought made me oddly grateful he hadn't. Some things were easier to see with objectivity. It was one of traits I had to learn from being my trade: emotional distance. You learned to look at death without letting it look back.

He gave me a long, knowing look, the kind that carried more than the words that followed. "Promise me you'll be careful."

I lifted my glass again, the wine catching in the kitchen light. "Why wouldn't I be careful?" I asked innocently.

FOUR

The morning after the carriage house fiasco, Liz and I showed up at the Historical Society headquarters like good little volunteers. The Society had made it clear that the Ghost Walk was not going to die just because a body had turned up where it was least convenient. Tragedy only slowed it down long enough for someone to print flyers about resilience. If the carriage house was off limits, then headquarters would have to do. They wanted hands to hang cobwebs and set up props.

Liz and I fit the part. Ordinary citizens helping out. Nothing suspicious about that, which made it the perfect cover for us to gather intel. We were there to smile, unpack boxes, and listen. Mostly listen. People always talked more when their hands were busy. Why ask when you could simply eavesdrop?

The moment we walked inside, the noise hit us. Headquarters was buzzing like a kicked anthill. Volunteers scurried across the floor with armfuls of boxes, ladders scraped against the walls, and every corner echoed with overlapping instructions no one was following. People were taping up paper bats, arguing over where to put the coffin prop, and generally mistaking chaos for progress.

The oak tables, usually polished and dignified, had vanished under a mountain of clutter. Rubber bats with chipped wings, candlesticks cemented with old wax, paper lanterns sagging like balloons. Mannequin limbs poked out from under one table. The heads were in another box, wigs sliding half off their scalps. Someone had labeled a banker's box "ARCHIVES" and filled it with fake plastic skulls. Another box read "DO NOT THROW OUT" and held three broken extension cords and a single glove.

If you squinted, the place looked less like the site of a haunting and more like the aftermath of a rummage sale that had gone badly wrong. But in Cheerville, enthusiasm mattered more than atmosphere. The Society wanted to sell a ghost story, and the town was eager to help out and make it happen. Liz wasn't the only one who needed something to do with her hands, even if it was just adding cobwebs around fake tombstones. It gave everyone busywork and a sense of purpose.

All the better for me. With so much noise and motion, no one paid attention to where I wandered or what I listened to. I moved in small circles, pausing just long enough to be helpful and long enough to overhear. Fiddling with a roll of tape got you a minute. Borrowing a step stool got you two. A broom in your hand practically made you invisible.

Near the window, two older ladies bent over the fog machine as though it were a patient on life support. I recognized Mrs. Crenshaw, who had once tried to rope me into her quilting circle. She still had the same air of authority, as if needles and thread gave her the right to dictate all matters mechanical. She and her companion debated the best way to store the machine even though they had only just taken it out. One insisted it had to go back into its original box or the motor would warp. The other swore it would be safer wrapped in a quilt, preferably one she had stitched herself. Neither looked likely to yield an inch. I half-expected them to call for a vote before anyone dared plug the thing in.

No one here could coordinate a bake sale

without a shouting match, yet somehow the town kept running. Maybe dysfunction was its own kind of order.

Across the room, Pauline had claimed a chair like a throne and stationed her cane beside her. Two nervous teenagers hovered at her elbow, folding programs under her exacting supervision. She corrected every crease with a sharp tap of her finger, snapping at them when the edges wandered even slightly. "Straighten the corners. No one wants a crooked souvenir," she barked, her voice carrying over the clatter of decorations.

If she'd been born in another century, she'd have been running a household staff or an army. Here, she ran the Historical Society's programs and folding tables.

Then her gaze found me. "Barbara. Fancy seeing you here. And Liz. Hi."

Before I could answer, Gretchen waddled past with her walker, her handlebars draped with a lopsided string of paper bats. She grinned broadly, unbothered by the chaos around her. "I told them if anything's missing, you'll track it down. You always do." The bats swung precariously as she shuffled on, leaving the faint scent of lavender powder in her wake.

"Don't let them use too much tape," she said. "Last year they taped a wreath to the church door and took the paint with it. Tape leaves marks."

"Duly noted," I said.

Liz lingered to chit-chat. My attention had shifted to the far corner, where two women leaned close together in whispered conversation. They must have thought they were being discreet, but their voices carried easily across the room. In less than thirty seconds I picked out three words: "embarrassment," "scandal," and "terrible for tourism."

It figured. If Cheerville could bottle its gossip and feed it into the power grid, the Historical Society would never pay another light bill.

I adjusted a plastic pumpkin on a nearby table and let their words float toward me. One of them, a woman with the rhinestone glasses, was insisting that Patrick's death had been handled poorly, though she couldn't say why. Another said she had heard it was connected to that boy who got into a bike accident last week. A third mused whether Patrick had been cursed by something associated with his antiques. The stories were already breeding like rabbits.

By the coffee urn, my neighbor Martha had established herself like royalty at court. She sat in a folding chair, her Styrofoam cup balanced neatly on her knee, and told her version of last night's discovery to anyone who wandered close enough to listen.

"Police everywhere," she announced, her voice pitched loud enough to carry over the chatter. "Lights flashing. Half the town saw it. Of course I knew something was wrong the moment they announced that carriage house stunt." She leaned forward for emphasis. "And mark my words, it's always the ones with the clean reputations. You just wait. There'll be something shady in his business dealings."

In Martha's telling, she had predicted the entire event and personally warned the mayor. Martha had never met a fact she couldn't adopt. She was Cheerville's one-woman news cycle: self-sourced, self-edited, and always confident.

Her audience nodded in rapture. Martha had a way of pinning people down with words. When her eyes landed on me, her whole face brightened as though she had just spotted the crown witness for her story. She lifted a hand in greeting, clearly expecting me to confirm her account.

I gave her a polite nod, one that neither confirmed nor denied, and kept moving before she could demand more. She would embellish her tale with or without me. By tomorrow, she'd have added motive and dialogue.

Liz caught up at my shoulder, her mouth tight with irritation. "This is worse than the debriefing room in Kandahar," she muttered, just low enough for me to hear.

She wasn't wrong. The whole building buzzed with nervous energy. Volunteers flitted across the floor like anxious bees, arms full of props, ladders screeching as they dragged them from wall to wall. Someone demanded to know where the coffin had gone. No one remembered who moved it. I did. I'd watched a pair of retirees roll it toward the archives door and block a fire exit with it. I didn't stop to share.

Liz stood easy, but her eyes moved in precise, methodical sweeps. I could see the old training in the way her gaze landed on each corner of the room, cataloguing every pile of boxes, every stack of paper programs, every restless volunteer. She noticed what others missed. The crooked chair leg, the door propped open a few inches too wide. Even here, she operated like someone who expected trouble to step out of the supply closet.

I smoothed my expression into something harmless. Smile, nod, keep your mouth shut. That was all it took to blend in, and I still needed to in order to get answers. Around here, a polite face and a willingness to stack chairs was better cover than a forged passport. People looked right past you if you gave them nothing to latch onto. A former mentor once told me the key to invisibility was purpose. Pretend you belonged, and you did.

I poured myself a coffee and drifted toward a table where two women were busy chatting and painting fake tombstones. Their brushes trembled with imprecision, distracted by the excitement only gossip could fuel.

"Such a shame about the carriage house," I offered, my tone mild. "And Patrick."

"Oh yes, dreadful," the first woman replied instantly, as though she had already repeated the line to half the county by breakfast. "Patrick was always so supportive."

Her friend leaned closer, her voice dropping half a note but not nearly enough to keep me from hearing. "And so adamant on what he wanted. He always insisted things be done properly."

"Do you think that got him in trouble?" I asked.

The first woman nodded, lips pressed into a thin line. "His passion wasn't always matched by others. Especially for those with different opinions."

"Such as?" I waited for details.

"For example, he insisted the carriage house be included. Pushed for it, really. I told him it was too much trouble."

"Gerald disagreed," the second cut in. "He said it was impractical. It was too far out of the way, and not worth the effort."

The first nodded. "He really didn't want to use the carriage house, but Patrick managed to convince the others."

That made me pause. I racked my brain for a Gerald in this town and came up blank. It was name I hadn't yet heard connected with the Ghost Walk. I let my voice come out light, almost careless. "Who's Gerald?"

The first woman blinked, surprised anyone could be so uninformed. "Gerald Whitlow," she said quickly, as though the name itself explained everything.

The second woman added, "You know. On the committee." She turned back to her brush, carefully tracing another letter while lowering her voice to what she probably thought was a whisper. "He's very involved. Always has opinions. Especially about how to make money."

"I don't know him," I said.

"You'd know him if you saw him," the first woman said.

The second nodded quickly, eager to add more. "Tall, neat, not a white hair out of place. I saw him arrive a minute ago." She craned her neck, scanning the room with exaggerated care. "Where did he go?"

I followed her gaze. Most of the volunteers looked rumpled, shoulders hunched, faces flushed from effort. In the sea of flannel shirts and sagging cardigans, not one of them resembled the polished figure she had just described. Most people around here dressed for comfort and called it charm.

The woman shrugged. "Must've disappeared."

I drifted back toward Liz, lowering my voice so it carried no farther than her ear. "Gerald Whitlow. Do you know him?"

She rolled her eyes. "He's on the committee," she said. "He's a big donor, so he thinks he's the boss." She tilted her chin toward the far end of the hall. "That's him."

My eyes swept past a cluster of retirees untangling string lights, to a man stepping away from a stack of boxes. He was tall with commanding posture. His hair was parted with surgical precision. His shirt was tucked so neatly it might have been pressed only moments before. Even in the chaos of the hall, where everyone else was sweating and red-faced, he moved like a man who believed himself above the noise.

"The one who looks like an oil tycoon?" I asked.

"Yup," Liz answered.

I clocked him immediately. I'd met his type before: men who smiled while measuring your usefulness to their agenda.

We weren't inconspicuous about observing him, and soon he was staring back at us. Liz gave him a fake smile and waved, and he smiled back, walking our way. As he approached, he smoothed a nonexistent wrinkle from his tie. He was a man who liked to be in control.

"Brace yourself," Liz murmured under her breath. "He's about to call me by name like we're lifelong friends."

"Liz," Gerald said as he approached. "I thought I recognized you. Good to see you pitching in to help out."

I caught the flicker of irritation in her eyes, but she suppressed it in favor of an abundance of politeness.

"Gerald." Liz nodded. "I was just telling my friend what a big help you've been on the committee."

I gave Liz my own fake smile while watching her perform. She was good at this. She was saying all this without any hint of irony. Her voice had that warm coat of community spirit. Maybe she should audition for the community theatre. She'd get the lead.

Gerald's smile sharpened, meant to charm but carried obvious calculation underneath. He clasped his hands together, pretending to be bashful about the praise. "Oh, I wouldn't say that," he said. "We all just do what we can."

"This is my friend Barbara," Liz said.

Gerald's gaze slid to me then, shaking his head slightly as though remembering his manners. "Yes. Nice to officially meet you, Barbara," he said. "I heard you were the one who found poor Patrick. What an ordeal for you both. It must've been quite the shock."

"It was...traumatic," I said, putting on my best scared face. My voice trembled just enough to sound believable.

"None of us expected anything like that," Liz said, breathless.

"Why would you?" Gerald replied, pouncing on the agreement as though it were a lifeline. "Who would? A man dies in the middle of our Ghost Walk preparations, of all things. It's terrible for his family.

Terrible for the town." His words rolled out as if he had rehearsed them for future retellings. He had the rhythm down too well, the pauses placed exactly where sympathy was meant to go.

Liz nodded. "Patrick was dedicated to this event. He put in a great deal of work."

"Yes. He certainly had opinions about how things should be done." The smile stayed, but I caught the jaw tightening. There was history there. His voice softened just a shade too late.

Before I could nod, Gerald leaned in to close the distance. His voice dropped from the register of casual conversation. "When you found him... you didn't see anyone else in the carriage house, did you?"

I met his eyes. "Not that I saw," I said at last. "Why?"

He shrugged a little too quickly, a rehearsed motion, meant to look easy but landing stiff instead. "Oh, no reason. Only that security around here is minimal. If the doors were unlocked, anyone could have slipped through."

The words were light, but his tone betrayed him. It was a tone of interrogation.

I caught the way Liz's gaze lingered on Gerald

for a beat longer than necessary. We both said nothing.

Gerald rushed to fill the silence. His smile brightened, teeth flashing. "Well, I am glad you had each other," he said smoothly. "Situations like that can leave quite an impression."

"Unsettling," I agreed.

"Yes. Exactly." His hand rose to smooth his tie again. The gesture, I realized, was more of a nervous tic.

Then, with the air of a man convinced he had tied the bow on a conversation neatly, he pivoted back toward the stack of boxes waiting in the corner. Even his exit was rehearsed: three steps, a courteous half-turn, one final smile to suggest closure.

People reveal themselves when they believe they were making small talk. Gerald Whitlow had just told me more than he realized.

His question lingered in my head. *You didn't see anyone else in the carriage house, did you?*

Who else could've been there?

FIVE

Gerald Whitlow's question made me wonder if there was something more to the carriage house, some detail I had walked past or dismissed. Maybe something that had been right in front of me the whole time.

His pretense of casualness had a weight that kept nudging at the back of my mind. People only asked if you had been alone when they wanted to know what you might have seen. If there were any more witnesses.

The police had already ruled Patrick's death a homicide. Rope burns across the wrists didn't leave much room for interpretation. But knowing something was murder and knowing why it happened were two very different things.

Grimal and his officers had handled it the way they always did. They had sealed off the scene with tape and padlocks, shuffled through their paperwork, and waited for the medical examiner to hand them confirmation of what they already suspected. By the time they finished, any small detail that mattered might already have been gone.

Gerald's remark made me too curious about what else could be hiding in the carriage house, things that the police might have missed too. Which was how I found myself back at the carriage house that night, cutting my dinner with my son's family short. I'd smiled, nodded in all the right places, and made my excuses that I was especially tired from volunteering earlier that day. Little did they know my night was only getting started.

The padlock Grimal's men had secured across the doors gleamed faintly in the dark, meant to reassure the public that the scene was sealed. To me, it was only a question waiting to be answered.

The October air had a sharpness to it that my black turtleneck did little to blunt against the cold. Behind me, the street carried the stillness of a small town at rest. The only sounds were leaves scraping across the pavement. While Cheerville slept, I stood awake listening.

I kept my movements small and silent just in case anyone was peeking from windows.

The carriage house loomed before me. It looked like what it had always been, an old building given historical status. But now I suspected it held secrets, waiting for someone to prod them loose.

The lock was simple, the sort you could buy at a hardware store. Still, I took my time with this one, careful not to make noise. The metal protested faintly, but after a minute there was a click. The shackle shifted under my hand and gave way.

I looked behind me one last time, my ears straining to hear any approaching footsteps on gravel. Nothing except the wind rustling fallen leaves and the soft rattle of branches scratching the roof.

Satisfied, I slipped the lock free and dropped it into my pocket. My hand found the door. The hinges resisted for a moment before yielding. I eased the door wider and stepped inside, careful to let it close behind me without a slam.

The air hit me first. It carried the must of old wood, but layered over it was the faint metallic tang of chemicals the police had sprayed. It was the smell of procedure: disinfectant, fingerprint powder, and something else faintly medicinal. It reminded me of morgues.

The lanterns still dangled from their hooks, their glow extinguished but their cords swaying faintly in the draft. Cobwebs still sagged in dusty ropes. And the Widow mannequin still stood bent in her eternal vigil, veil drooping. But the theatrical clutter collided with the blunt fact of death. A strip of police tape cut across the alcove, and before me was the chalk outline of where I'd last seen Patrick Halloway.

The outline looked smaller than I remembered him. Death always shrank people somehow. It pressed them flat, took away the angles and dimensions that made them human. Even the props seemed to keep their distance now, as if ashamed of their earlier performance.

The carriage house now had a strange double life: half haunted house attraction, half crime scene. It was as if the Widow herself were playing hostess, offering guests a tour of both stories at once.

I had seen worse in my time. Birthday banners still hanging above walls pocked with bullet holes. Wedding flowers trampled into mud on a battlefield. Theatrics and violence always seemed to find one another. One was built to distract, the other to erase. First came the show, and then came the ruin.

I moved carefully, my eyes traveling across the markers Grimal's team had left behind. Neat little triangles announcing what they thought was worth noting: a scuff in the wood near the alcove, a fiber caught on a nail, a faint drag line etched into the dust where Patrick's body had been pulled.

I pulled a small flashlight from my pouch and clicked it on, shielding the beam with my hand until it was narrowed to a thin glow. A controlled strip along the floor was enough. The beam was tight, disciplined light, small enough to hide, strong enough to expose.

I started slow. First the alcove, where the tape still hung limp across the opening. I shifted the light, letting it crawl across the fake gravestones stacked carelessly in one corner. They looked even cheaper under inspection. Paint flaking, foam edges dented. Nothing worth noting. The beam skimmed across a scatter of paper bats that had fallen during the police sweep. Their wings twitched faintly in the draft.

The Widow's mannequin loomed like a bored witness. She was still grieving over her husband to cry about anyone else. The rafters above were still dressed in cobwebs. In the corner, the fog machine squatted like an abandoned animal, its cord coiled at its feet.

I let the beam drop back to the boards beneath me. They were darkened with age, warped and swollen from damp. The nail heads had rusted over. But I kept the light steady.

That was when I saw it.

A short row in the middle looked wrong. The color was close, but the surface was too neat. Someone had scuffed it to match, but the pattern was deliberate, not the haphazard scarring of time. I bent lower, narrowing the beam further, letting it slide across the seams. The edges were sharp, and the grain looked cleaner than the boards around it.

It was their uniformity that stood out. Wood that old didn't age politely. It chipped and split in odd places. But these boards seemed to have manners. They wanted to blend in, and almost worked.

I pressed my fingertips against one. The wood was firm, but not softened like the rest. They were not decades old. They were fairly new. Months, maybe less.

I angled the light. My eyes hunted for nail heads. There were none on these planks. What looked like nail marks were nothing more than dark stains, painted in to fool a quick glance. Viewed from above, it passed well enough. To a casual glance, even to a police team searching for evidence, it looked like honest repair work. But under my hand, the truth announced itself. These boards had been laid here to be easy to lift.

I shifted my weight carefully, placing my heel squarely on the edge of one plank. If it had been nailed tight like the others, the board would have resisted, groaning against the pressure. Instead, it gave a little under my weight, flexing just enough for the other end to lift.

I could feel the air beneath it shift, faint but present. The floor was pretending to be solid, and I had just caught it in the lie.

I tried again, shifting my heel to another corner. The result was the same: the surface dipped, not far, but enough to tell me the section was floating rather than fixed. Whoever set these boards down had cut them to fit like a lid across the opening.

I stepped back slowly and widened the flashlight beam. The light washed across the entire section, showing it as one piece now. Four boards across, three deep.

I pressed my heel down on the edge of one plank again, then bent down to grasp the other end that had risen. As I figured, the whole section lifted up in unison. It rose without protest.

Beneath it sat a trapdoor. The iron handle lay flat against the surface.

The metal caught the light coming from the window and threw it back weakly, dulled by years of use. I set the planks aside and crouched over the hidden door, the flashlight beam catching the faint scratches around the ring where others had lifted it before. There were faint smudges where fingers had pressed, the marks of repetition. Whoever used it did so regularly.

I wrapped my gloved fingers around the iron ring and opened it.

The opening gaped at my feet, darker than any corner of the room. My flashlight beam dropped straight down, but the light dissolved almost immediately, swallowed whole by the black. It looked like an endless pit, a drop into nothing.

I held the beam steady, waiting for it to find a bottom. My eyes strained, but the dark didn't return the courtesy. It absorbed everything. It seemed to mock my light for even trying.

I crouched lower, and angled the beam around. This time, the light caught something. A narrow strip of iron flashed back at me. I moved the beam slightly and saw another, just below it. A line of dull glints repeating themselves into the dark.

I counted without meaning to and stopped only when the rungs blurred into shadow. The black swallowed everything past a certain point. But it was clear that this was a ladder. The rungs ran straight down, bolted into the wall with thick brackets. I reached out and brushed it lightly with my glove. It was not new, but not crumbling either. This wasn't decoration or some relic from history. This had been built for use, and it had been built to last.

The metal was cool, not surprising, since it never saw sunlight. The bolts were tight, and not rusted through, and the rungs showed the faint polish from regular use.

I stayed still and listened. I thought I had heard something down below. Not voices I could pin down, but a vibration, maybe. Rats scuttling? It was vague enough to keep me questioning whether I had heard anything at all.

Sound traveled differently underground. The first rule of covert listening: never trust an echo. I waited through three breaths before deciding it was nothing. Or nothing yet.

I leaned back slightly, steadying my grip on the flashlight. The draft that rose out of the opening curled around my ankles, colder than the rest of the room. It felt less like moving air and more like breath, as if the space itself was exhaling in relief of being discovered. The air touched my face like it was testing me back.

The Widow of Whitcomb Hill came to mind before I could stop it. The story had been told so many times it lived in the bones of this place. The weeping wife, veil trailing, her cries carrying on as she searched for her lost husband.

I didn't believe in ghosts, never had. I'd seen too much of what flesh and blood could do to put stock in shadows. Yet crouched here with the cold draft curling upward and the ladder dropping away into dark, I could understand why the story had survived so long.

Superstition had its uses. It keeps curious children from wandering into danger, and it gave adults an explanation when something awful didn't have a logical reason. Legends grew around practical truths like ivy around a fencepost. The story distracted the townspeople, while the real secret lay beneath their feet, waiting for someone bold or foolish enough to lift the lid. Tonight, that someone was me.

Foolishness and boldness share a border so thin I've crossed it plenty of times without realizing until it was too late. Still, this was what I did best, find the things other people walked past.

Ghosts didn't build ladders. People did. And if

this ladder led somewhere, then someone in Cheerville already knew exactly where it went. That meant they were either protecting it or profiting from it, probably both.

The question was whether I should go after it now or later, when I had more supplies.

I was prepared to take a few steps down, enough to taste the air, measure the sound, decide whether the way forward was worth it. My instincts told me to retreat, regroup, and then return with the right tools. But I was already here, and I was curious. I might have discovered the legendary tunnels, and I wanted to know if that was true.

Still undecided, I shifted closer, but that was when I heard it, clearer this time. Not the whistle of wind through stone, but actual voices.

It was too muffled for me to make out the words, but clear enough not to mistake for anything else. Men's voices, talking to one another.

One laughed, which echoed. The other answered in a tone that didn't rise or fall.

I turned off my flashlight and listened. Darkness dropped down over me like a hood. My eyes strained for detail, but the only glow came from the faint cracks in the boards above, a reminder that the world outside was still there.

My breath fogged against the cold air rising from the opening. The voices swelled again, louder this time, though still indistinct. But they were closer now. The scrape of movement carried with them. I felt the faint tremor of footsteps climbing somewhere below.

Whoever they were, at least one of them was climbing up the ladder with the confidence of doing so many times before.

I lowered myself back onto my heels, keeping as still as stone. Whatever curiosity had urged me to test the ladder was gone. Someone was down there, a man, maybe more than one person. And they were moving quickly.

Curiosity was an asset, but tonight it was a liability. Slowly and carefully, I closed the door to a quiet close. Whoever was climbing up was coming closer. I had to get out of here.

The trick was to make the place look untouched. I didn't want this person to know someone other than the police had been here. My hands moved on memory. I replaced the boards exactly as they had been.

I crossed the floor without hurry, my steps chosen for quiet. The door gave a long groan as I pushed it open, and I slipped out. I refitted the lock, guiding the shackle back into place until it clicked shut. The sound cracked the silence of the street like a stone dropped into still water.

Too loud, I thought immediately. I stepped back, letting the night reabsorb me. The cold air on my face felt cleaner than the air inside. I stepped back into the shadows of a tree at the edge of the property and waited.

SIX

The thing about secrets was that they could never stay buried for long. You could pile all the dirt you wanted on top of them, but sooner or later they wriggled free, hungry for daylight. Some came quietly, while others made a mess in their return. Either way, they surfaced. And if the carriage house had another way out, I intended to find it.

I'd seen governments try to contain scandals with paperwork, agents try to hide assets with aliases, lovers try to disguise betrayals with smiles. It all ended the same way, with the truth swelling up until it cracked through the surface. This was no different, although this was a secret pretending to be folklore.

The street was still with a silent heaviness. The air was sharp enough to sting when I drew a breath. I stayed low behind the trunk of a maple, feeling the bark rough against my palms. As I waited in the shadows, the only light came from a streetlamp that cast its weak yellow circle across the pavement, making everything beyond it sink deeper into black. I blended in, just another shape in the dark.

Grimal's padlock caught the glow, winking faintly each time the wind stirred the branches above. Officially, the place was sealed. I knew better. If someone was coming up from the tunnels, or whatever was down there, they wouldn't be able to get out from the front. There had to be another exit. Had I known about it earlier, I would have used it myself.

The police loved barriers that looked like authority. Real professionals used barriers that didn't look like anything at all. Whoever had access to that passage and knew their way around wouldn't go to all that trouble just to be locked inside with a chalk outline. There had to be another door.

It was one of the oldest rules in the book: where there was a way down, there was always a way out. Smugglers, spies, and criminals all shared that much in common. They wouldn't dig themselves into a hole without practical exits. I'd seen enough safehouses to know that they had more than one escape route.

The seconds dragged, but waiting came easily to me. It always had. I shifted my weight slightly behind the trunk, careful not to crunch the leaves beneath my shoes. My eyes stayed fixed on the carriage house, tracing every dark window, every line of siding, committing the shape of the place to memory. Most people grew impatient after five minutes. I could wait for hours if the situation demanded it. The night made me alert. It had taught me patience.

Then, faintly, from inside the carriage house came the sound of something being moved. The hidden door, likely, moving the panel of planks. Then came a sound so faint it might have been nothing at all. The low groan of wood under strain, quiet enough that anyone else would have mistaken it for the building settling in the cold. But I knew the difference. This was movement, and it came from the side window, not the door.

My pulse slowed, not sped. That was always the giveaway my body communicated to me: when the danger got close, I got calm.

I leaned forward to see better, careful to keep my outline hidden in the dark. One of the windows had shifted oddly. It had not opened by the pane the way it should have. The entire frame had been pushed outward, creating a gap wide enough for a person to slip through.

The motion had been subtle, and it would've gone unnoticed unless you were looking for it. At first glance, the man who climbed out was nothing remarkable. Medium height, thinning hair, wearing a plain dark jacket. He looked harmless in appearance. He was the type you could stand behind in the grocery line for years and never recognize again.

He was built for invisibility. Average height, average clothes, average face, the perfect camouflage. The ones who could vanish in a crowd without ever moving faster than a walk made the best agents.

But the way he moved gave him away. He rolled out of the window with practiced ease, landing neatly and quietly on his feet, like a cat. This was not the first time he had done it.

His weight distribution was perfect: heels absorbing the fall, center of gravity steady, shoulders relaxed. His hands never touched the frame for balance. His knees absorbed the drop cleanly. Even the way he didn't pause to adjust his jacket had the economy of someone who didn't waste movements. My gut tightened. This was a professional.

The smallest tells betrayed training: no flinching, no self-correction, no hesitation. I could almost see the muscle memory in him. Someone like that didn't panic, and never left evidence on purpose. Witnesses neither.

He swept the street with his eyes in one smooth motion from left to right. Satisfied, he brushed his palms together, then started down the sidewalk at a measured pace. There was no need for him to run or hurry. Any more speed or movement might've roused suspicion.

I slipped from my place behind the trunk and fell in behind him, matching his rhythm from across the street. The trick was to move when he moved and stop when he stopped. Unfortunately, Cheerville was not built for surveillance. The sidewalks were wide, the trees sparse, and the quiet made every step sound louder than it should have. Even the moon felt intrusive, washing the street in a pale light that flattened shadows. It reminded me of the difference between city work and small-town work. In a city, you could blend into a crowd of a thousand. Here, a squirrel could cough wrong and give you away. I had to keep my distance, far enough to stay invisible, close enough not to lose him.

The hunt had begun.

There was a particular calm that settled in me once a pursuit started. Every sense heightened, every instinct aligned. It was less adrenaline and more mathematics: distance, light, timing, cover. I'd forgotten how natural it still felt to use these skills.

We moved through the neighborhood in near silence. When the street widened into the main part of town, the change worked in my favor. Shopfronts lined the sidewalks, all dark and shuttered. The wider streets and narrow alleys gave me more options for cover.

The display windows became mirrors, soft and warped, but useful enough. A reflection here, a silhouette there. I kept my eyes on the glass instead of his back. That was how you followed without being caught, by watching indirectly. You learned to see through the periphery.

I slipped into a rhythm that made me feel nostalgic. It was like speaking a language I hadn't spoken in a while. My senses sharpened with every step, the night air electric against my skin.

The street looked so ordinary and innocent, oblivious to danger simmering. Somewhere, a dog barked once and went quiet. Maybe the dog could sense it.

The bland man kept his rhythm unbroken, until he stopped to light a cigarette. He drew once, exhaled, and continued on without looking back.

The glow of the cigarette had been brief, a single orange flicker in the dark, but I caught enough of it to mark the angle of his jaw, clean-shaven. He didn't have the look of someone sleeping rough. His clothes were clean, shoes dark to disguise any dirt or mud. A professional didn't neglect the details that keep him unnoticed.

Once he was done with his cigarette, he threw the butt into the gutter without breaking stride. Even his smoke break was controlled. No fiddling with the lighter or unnecessary movements. But I could tell he wasn't strolling around town for the scenery. He was going somewhere.

As he moved, I began cataloguing details automatically. Right-handed smoker. Decent cardiovascular fitness, judging by his steady pace. Local or someone who knew the terrain well: he navigated the cracked sidewalks without hesitation, avoiding the loose slabs that tended to clack underfoot. That was a Cheerville trick. Tourists never learned it. If I hadn't noticed him, this was a man who had practiced the art of being invisible.

He didn't check his phone or glance in windows. He didn't flinch at the buzz of a streetlight or the bark of a distant dog. His focus stayed forward. The discipline reminded me of the men I used to trail across borders, contractors who made themselves ghosts by routine alone.

The second break came without warning. One instant he was moving, the next he wasn't. He stopped mid-step, turned, and scanned the street behind him. His instincts were sharp. He hadn't heard me, I was certain, but some internal alarm had gone off.

Maybe it was a reflection caught too long in a window. Or maybe he just had that sixth sense that grew in people who've been followed before. Whatever it was, his posture shifted from relaxed to alert.

Luckily I had stayed close against the wall of a shop, and as soon as he turned, I slipped into the narrow alley beside it. My stomach tightened. He was onto me.

My movements were instinctive. My body remembered how to disappear before my mind even caught up. The muscles in my back flattened against brick, breath locked behind my teeth. I hadn't done this in a while, but apparently, retirement didn't erase training. It just hid under cardigans.

The alley was cramped, lined with brick slick from condensation. The ground was littered with damp leaves that clung to the soles of my shoes. A heavy business trash bin sat wedged against one wall, one of those wheeled plastic dumpsters with a lid that never closed right. It smelled faintly of grease and old coffee. I crouched low behind it, steadying my breathing.

His footsteps slowly came closer. I could hear him stop at the mouth of the alley, and I knew that his eyes were sweeping the dark, calculating whether it hid anyone. I pressed tighter against the bin, spine rigid against the cold brick, every muscle tight. My breaths came slow and controlled, each one measured so it made no sound.

I pictured his line of sight the way I'd taught recruits to do: center scan, corner check, backlight silhouette. If he stepped three feet in, he'd see the faint edge of my body. Two more and he'd hear me shift my weight. I thought briefly about the Glock tucked in my nightstand at home and cursed the optimism that made me leave it there.

Moments like this stretched time. A second felt like a minute. The scrape of his steps shifted closer, then stopped. He was standing right in front of the trash bin now. His instincts were right. He knew he was not alone.

He wasn't breathing hard, which told me he wasn't scared, just curious. A hunter's stillness. My fingers brushed the edge of a loose lid. If I needed to,

I could knock it over, make noise, run. But running was what amateurs did. I waited.

And then, from nowhere, salvation. A cat slipped out from beneath the trash bin.

It yowled once, stretching like it had all the time in the world, tail flickering. Through the narrow crack between the bin and the wall, I watched him stiffen. The cat paused mid-street, turned, and fixed him with those unblinking, reflective eyes. It gave a small, unimpressed mewl. The man shifted and exhaled a laugh under his breath. I let the relief wash through me. The cat glanced back once, eyes glinting gold in the lamplight. It reminded me of Dandelion.

The cat mewed again as if scolding him for interrupting its evening stroll. The man let out a noise that could have been a laugh or a snort. He shook his head, muttered something too low to catch, and turned back toward the street. His steady footsteps resumed, the sound fading as he returned to his rhythm.

I stayed where I was until the echo of his boots was gone. Only then did I rise from behind the bin, my knees protesting as I stretched my stiff legs. The air outside the alley felt fresher. By the time I reached the end of the block, he was gone. He had vanished as cleanly as he had come out of the window.

The street lay open before me, harmless again. Shopfronts reflected nothing but the faint glow of the streetlamps, and the only motion came from a banner overhead twitching in the breeze. My eyes swept the doors and windows of the storefronts. Had he slipped into one of them? Was he watching me now? I turned in a slow circle, checking every direction out of habit. All empty.

Just like that, the bland man had been erased from the night. Either he was long gone, or he knew how to blend better than I'd given him credit for.

I stood there for a long moment, breathing slowly. The image of him dropping from the carriage house window replayed itself in my mind. If he knew the town this well and could navigate it without second-guessing, either someone powerful had hired him to be here, or he was working for himself. Neither possibility comforted me. Whoever he was, he was definitely not a harmless committee volunteer. He was trained and dangerous.

And he had nerve. To crawl through the tunnels, surface in the middle of a police investigation, and walk the streets like it was just another night, well, that that kind of calm didn't come cheap. Whoever he worked for, they weren't small-time smugglers hawking antiques out of a barn. It meant trouble was growing under Cheerville, and no one had noticed but me. Maybe it had taken root long before I came here.

But tonight, I owed a stray cat more thanks than I cared to admit. The creature had vanished too, leaving no trace but a few paw prints in the dew.

SEVEN

I woke feeling stiff, which came as no surprise. My knees ached from crouching, my muscles throbbed from pressing against cold brick, and a deep knot had taken up residence in the side of my neck. That was the cost of waiting behind trees and in alleys at my age.

There was a time when I could hold a position for hours and walk away without noticing it. Now, my body sent me the bill before sunrise. While the mind might stay sharp, the frame carrying it had its limits. I could outsmart most people in Cheerville, but outrunning them was another matter.

I sat on the edge of the bed, feet flat to the floor, and gave everything a brief inventory. Ankles rolled, wrists flexed, and fingers bent. I treated the stiffness like a briefing: acknowledge the data, make the adjustments, proceed. At least the machinery still worked. Function over comfort. That had always been my measure. As long as I could move, I could work.

A faint crack echoed through my right leg as I stretched for my slippers. It wasn't exactly pain, just the audible reminder that my body had a long memory. Last night's crouch behind the trash bin had left another imprint.

On the whole, I still felt like the woman I used to be, who could vanish into a crowd in Berlin or slip through a checkpoint in the Middle East without a second glance. Now I blended into church bake sales and garden clubs. Different camouflage, same purpose.

The hallway mirror caught me on my way past and offered its opinion without mercy. Hair sticking out at uneven angles, eyes puffy from too little sleep, skin a shade paler than usual. I had looked worse, and in worse places. Nothing a splash of cold water and enough coffee couldn't cure.

In the bathroom, the water hit icy, and I welcomed it. It shocked the fog out of my head. A few minutes later I had pulled on a thick sweater, the one soft enough to trick my shoulders into loosening, and padded toward the kitchen. The house was silent except for the steady tick of the hallway clock and the low hum of the refrigerator. Morning light edged through the blinds, turning the counters silver.

Dandelion appeared just long enough to brush against my leg, tail high, demanding breakfast before retreating to his sunspot by the window. He didn't care about dead bodies, smugglers, or secret tunnels. His world revolved around punctual meals and warm surfaces. I poured cat food into his bowl, and then I made coffee.

I stood over the sink while the steam curled into my face. The first sip burned the back of my throat and started the long process of turning me human again. The stiffness in my joints began to ease, not gone but quieted and manageable.

Lately, I'd been taking my caffeine black, no sugar. The bitterness cleared the mind better than meditation ever could. I let the warmth of the mug settle into my palms until my mind caught up with the rest of me.

On the kitchen table sat my notebook, left open from the night before. I had written in it after midnight. Not a full account, but just enough notes to keep the memory from slipping. If I'd been back in the field, I would have kept an encrypted file, but now that it wasn't necessary, I used a ballpoint pen and a college-ruled notebook, keeping my thoughts between grocery lists and cookie recipes.

I sat down and flipped back to read what I had managed to record. A few short lines on the man: ordinary, almost forgettable face. Mid-forties. Dark clothes. The ease with which he rolled out of the carriage house window and landed without a sound. How he had vanished in town just as quickly.

What I didn't write down was my unease. He had strong gut instincts that rivalled mine. I still didn't discount that he might have been hiding somewhere after he disappeared on the street, watching me. And he was out there now somewhere in Cheerville, calm, deadly, and planning his next move.

I drew a long breath and uncapped my pen. I turned to a fresh page. I recounted all the important details so far.

• *Patrick Halloway. Local antiques dealer. Committee volunteer. Found dead in carriage house prop. Rope burns.*

• *Gerald Whitlow. Committee volunteer. Huge donor. Asked if we were alone in carriage house.*

• *Carriage house: floorboards lifted. Trap door underneath. Likely leading to tunnels. Voices below.*

• *Man slipped out window. Nondescript features. Trained. Knew he was being followed.*

I tapped the pen against the page, staring at the list. A dead antiques dealer. A suspicious donor. Hidden tunnels. And a trained man moving through town like he owned the night. I needed to find a line that would connect them all.

Patrick was dead. That was fact. The tunnels existed. Another fact. At least one person knew about the tunnels. I'd bet the bland man wasn't working alone. Men like that didn't crawl through trapdoors for fun. The tunnels were likely an active route. Active routes always meant active players. I wondered how much contraband they had moved, and many dead bodies had been down there. Were *still* down there.

I closed the notebook and reached for my coffee again. The first sip was halfway to my lips when the phone rang. I set the cup down and checked the screen. It was Liz.

My thumb hovered a moment before I answered. Liz rarely made phone calls. She barely liked texting.

"Good morning," I said, though I already knew she wasn't calling for pleasantries.

"Barbara." Her voice was clipped. "They found Tyler early this morning."

That made me sit straighter. "Dead?"

"No. But nearly."

"Where?"

"In the Historical Society parking lot," she said. "He was lying there, unconscious. He's alive, but he hasn't woken up yet. The doctors are calling it a coma."

"Why?"

"That's what everyone's asking," Liz said. "I don't have all the details yet. Some people are saying he got in a fight, or got mugged, but you know how they run with gossip around here."

I sighed, knowing the theories would multiply like flies by lunchtime.

"Whatever it was, it doesn't sound accidental," I said.

"Right," Liz said. "Almost like they wanted him to be discovered."

That line prickled at me. Maybe someone was sending a message to the Historical Society. Then again, remembering the slick Gerald Whitlow, whoever had hurt Tyler was already a member of the Historical Society.

"Any witnesses?" I asked. "Someone must have seen something."

"Not really. The report came from a woman

walking her dog. She thought he was drunk at first, then realized it was Tyler. I haven't heard anything beyond that."

I could picture it, Tyler stretched out under a flickering lamp. "Do you know what he was even doing there?"

"No," Liz said. "I assume he was at the Society to finish up some work. Maybe he stayed later than the other volunteers."

Or someone had lured him there, or he'd found something intriguing in the building that made him stay that late. Either way, he wasn't the kind of boy who got into street fights to end up comatose.

"He knew too much," I muttered, thinking about the tunnels.

"Maybe," Liz said. "He always had his nose in the records, asking about old maps. But if he found something useful, he didn't tell me. Anyway, I'm going to the Society now to get more information. I can't visit him at the hospital because they're only allowing family. But he's in a coma anyway."

"Let me know what you find," I said. "Try to sift the gossip from the facts."

She snorted. "That's going to be hard." Then her tone dropped lower. "Things are getting weird around here."

"It's not a coincidence," I said, "Tyler's accident. I'm sure it's all connected."

I thought about telling Liz about the tunnels, but I decided to wait. I wanted confirmation first, by going down there myself. And I also knew someone who might have something more to share about Tyler.

Tyler had spent time with Octavian recently, talking through old smuggling legends and the Whitcomb ghost stories to weave them together into a script for the Ghost Walk. It had sounded harmless at the time, but maybe he had started looking too closely.

Tyler had too much curiosity. He was also too open and too trusting. He thought if a story was interesting, everyone would want to hear it. Some stories, though, were meant to stay untold.

If Tyler had stumbled onto a town secret, like the tunnels, and if he had talked about it with the wrong person, then someone had a good reason to put him out of the way. Gerald Whitlow? The bland man I had followed? Or maybe someone else entirely? Tyler had been talking to the whole Historical Society about his theories, maybe more locals outside of the committee too.

Octavian had a good memory for detail. If Tyler

had been excited, if he had said anything unusual, Octavian would remember it.

Seven minutes later, I had parked on Octavian's street. He was out front, sleeves rolled neatly to his elbows, pushing the mower across the yard. He looked happy and calm. He must not have heard about Tyler yet.

The neighborhood was still waking up. A few curtains twitched, a dog barked in the distance, and the scent of cut grass drifted on the crisp air. It was hard to believe that somewhere beneath this sleepy surface, a web of tunnels ran like hidden arteries. Up here, people were trimming hedges and talking about weekend plans. Down there, men were using those tunnels for something worth killing over.

I stepped out of the car and closed the door behind me. The mower's engine still hummed, and I waited until he noticed me rather than waving him down. When his eyes caught mine, he cut the engine and wiped his forehead with the back of his hand. He straightened, and his expression softened into a smile.

"Barbara," he said. "You could have called. I would've spared you the trip."

"Unfortunately, this isn't a social call," I answered.

The smile faded from his face as quickly as it had appeared. "What happened?"

"Tyler's in the hospital."

He froze, one hand still resting on the mower handle. For a moment, his eyes didn't move. The words hadn't finished sinking in. Then his knuckles whitened around the handle.

"*What?*"

"Liz phoned me this morning," I said. "They found him unconscious in the Historical Society parking lot. He hasn't woken up. He's in a coma."

He just stared at me as the weight of the words settled into place. "But... how? Why?"

"I think someone put him there."

"But that boy is earnest to a fault. He wouldn't have gone looking for trouble."

"Maybe trouble found him. Listen, I want to ask you some things."

He gestured to the chairs on the porch. I followed him up the steps, and we sat.

The lawn stretched out before us, half of it freshly cut. He studied it as though the order he had carved into the grass could line up into an answer.

"You've been spending time with him," I said, "training for the Ghost Walk. What has he said about the tunnels?"

Octavian leaned back in his chair. He didn't rush his answer. That was his way when he wanted to be precise. "He had a lot of theories. Lots of people assume that if the tunnels had been real, they've already collapsed, but Tyler thought they were still intact and running. He was convinced they were still down there."

He paused, glancing at me as if checking whether I'd laugh or dismiss it. I didn't.

"And he would tell anyone who would listen?"

Octavian nodded. "It was his passion, and he made it his mission to discover the tunnels."

"Was he close?" I asked.

Octavian shrugged. "Well, he'd been piecing things together. He found cellar maps in the archives, dug up old property records, even noted mentions of old storage shafts. He kept tracing routes that pointed toward the river. He said if you lined up the records carefully enough, you could see where they might have run." He let out a slow breath, his arms tightening against his chest. "He hadn't proven it yet, but he thought he was getting somewhere, especially since the Historical Society opened up some of the archives to the public last month."

"They did? Why?"

"They had a vote and decided it would be good for getting more donations from the public."

"I wonder what Gerald Whitlow thought about it," I muttered.

"Who?"

"Someone on the committee."

"I don't know him, but I heard some committee members were opposed to it. They had a vote about the decision." He looked at me sideways. "Barbara, do you believe the tunnels exist?"

I wanted to tell him about my discovery, but I couldn't rope Octavian into this. "Who knows," I said casually. "It matters what Tyler believed."

He nodded slowly, still studying me. Maybe he sensed there was more I wasn't saying, but he didn't press. That was one of his better qualities. He knew when to stop asking questions. It was one of the reasons we'd lasted this long.

"Well, Tyler also talked a lot about ghosts. He really believes in them. He said the tunnels were haunted, maybe even lined with the bodies of smugglers and bootleggers who never made it out. We were planning to weave those stories into his tours." He shook his head sadly.

"Even if he's right," I said, "the living are often more dangerous than the dead."

EIGHT

Cheerville thrived on its stories. Ghosts, smugglers, secret tunnels. They were safe entertainment that gave the town its charm. The idea of a whole hidden network under Cheerville was silly fun that most of the town embraced as legend but dismissed as nonsense. That was the way it was supposed to work, until someone started believing too much of it. Once someone started digging for facts, the ground shifted.

People loved fiction, but facts made people uncomfortable. Fictions were malleable and fun. That was why the town liked its ghosts tidy and ticketed. Tyler didn't treat the tunnels as entertaining folklore. He really believed in the tunnels. He seemed to have treated it like a quest for buried treasure. He must've found it, or gotten close enough to the truth to be threatening, because why else would he end up in the hospital? Was that why Patrick Halloway died?

Patrick had been left in the carriage house, and Tyler in the parking lot of the Historical Society. Both connected to the Society. Was someone really trying to send a message? Or did the perpetrator or perpetrators act in the heat of the moment before making hasty decisions and a quick getaway?

Maybe Tyler found a map and mentioned it to the wrong person. Maybe he bragged. Maybe amongst the people he bragged to was the bland man. Someone like Gerald Whitlow wouldn't get his hands dirty by knocking around a kid, but the bland man would without hesitation.

In my experience, clean operations left nothing behind. Whoever was behind this was organized enough, but not infallible. If they intended to send a warning, they did a poor job of it. This looked like a rushed job, done out of reaction rather than clear foresight. That meant there were cracks I could exploit.

All I knew was that I needed to go back to the carriage house. The only way forward was down. In the tunnels was where I would get more answers. If I wanted to know who was running things, I had to sneak into their hiding place. I clapped my hands together, excited about the prospect of what I would find down there.

So I spent the afternoon getting ready the way I always did. Practical gear lined the kitchen table while I picked the necessities. Clothes from the back of the closet, all black for the obvious reasons. A skin-tight top and trousers with pockets in the right places. I dug the balaclava out of the back of a drawer.

I packed a small bag with the economy of someone who has learned over the years what mattered and what was dead weight. One spare battery. A small roll of zip ties. A cheap pry bar with a wooden handle. A tiny first-aid kit with antiseptic and a few bandages. Not all of it was glamorous, but it was all useful.

I checked the pistol because I always check the pistol. The gun was clean, sighted, and loaded. Compact nine-millimeter, Glock 19-style. Nothing flashy, just reliable. I ran my thumb along the grip, a small ritual that settled my hands. If the gun ever left its holster, it would be because I had no other choice.

A small tracker the size of a coin went into a small outer pocket of the bag. If I found something worth following, I could track it.

Most importantly, I took a headlamp, which was an adjustable flashlight worn on an elastic strap around the head, leaving my hands free, though I had the flashlight on my phone as backup. I made sure my phone was fully charged too. I put thin work gloves in one pocket.

Light and hand protection were important underground. You wouldn't want to be balancing a torch while trying to climb a ladder. You wouldn't want bare skin to catch on wood splinters or nails or whatever was down there.

I checked everything twice out of muscle memory. Missions went sideways when the proper gear was forgotten. When I was sure I was properly packed, I was ready.

I filled Dandelion's bowls with food and water in case I didn't return by breakfast. Then I locked the door and stepped out into the evening.

Before long, I was back at the carriage house, but I didn't waste a glance on the front door. The bland man had already taught me that much. He'd gone through the window, and I would do the same again.

The houses at the far end were quiet and mostly darkened. A single porch light flickered in one house, but the curtains were closed. No one was looking. I walked toward the window.

The board yielded with the tired sigh of old wood, but it didn't give me trouble.

I slipped through, catching myself against the sill. The air inside still smelled faintly of disinfectant, and of course, the usual old wood and dust, stilled by the cold that lived in its old bones.

I let my eyes adjust so I wouldn't need to use the flashlight. The darkness wasn't absolute. A slice of moonlight came through a window and traced a thin silver edge across the wall. I remembered where the loose boards were. The Widow mannequin seemed to have shifted a little closer to the trapdoor, though I knew that was only a bit of my nerves mixed with excitement doing geometry.

The seam lifted under my hands. The panel came up as a single piece. I set the panel aside and opened the trapdoor. I pulled the balaclava down so only my eyes showed. The pistol was secure and quiet against my hip. I put on my headlamp and turned it on.

Light expanded in a tight white cone, cutting through the dark like a blade. The beam trembled slightly with my breathing before it steadied. I could hear my own pulse in my ears. This was what I used to call the threshold moment, when your mind tried to decide whether to listen to reason or instinct. I had learned to listen to both.

The ladder was cool under my gloves. I eased onto the first rung and felt it take my weight without complaint. The metal felt slick, maybe from moisture, maybe from use. Someone had climbed it recently, after all.

I moved down deliberately, counting my breaths as much as the rungs. Foot, hand, foot. The air grew tighter, the smell of river stronger, and I got the sense I was leaving my old life behind the deeper I went. The Barbara who ran errands and folded laundry stayed topside. The one who descended ladders in the dark was someone most of Cheerville didn't know existed.

My headlamp now made a small, steady circle that moved down with me step by step. Stone walls closed in on either side. Spider silk caught the beam like thread. I brushed one web aside and felt it cling to my sleeve, a ghost's handshake. Dust floated in the faint light like a slow snowfall.

Sound did strange things down here. A drip echoed somewhere as loud as a bell. My breath sounded loud until I slowed it. Slow breathing kept you steady. Being steady kept you alive.

The trick was to keep the mind quiet, too. Darkness fed on imagination, and imagination invented threats faster than reality did. I told myself that every unexplained sound, every shift of air, was just physics doing what it always had.

When I finally climbed down the last rung of the ladder, my boots sank into damp ground. The tunnel bent almost immediately, narrowing until the walls pressed close enough to make me crouch. The air was definitely colder down here. I adjusted the headlamp and let its beam drift ahead, tracing the curve of the passage.

I moved slowly. The walls were scarred with old pick marks. A thin layer of moisture clung to the stone, catching the light in slick glints like the skin of something alive.

Here and there, bits of wood jutted from the walls, the remains of supports that had once held the passage open. Some had rotted away completely. I imagined the sound of one breaking, and imagined the sudden rush of collapse. I forced my thoughts back to the present.

I kept walking until the tunnel went straight forward again. That was when I saw her.

At first, she didn't register as anything solid. For a second, I tried to convince myself it was a trick of the headlamp light bouncing off uneven stone. She was as dark as a shadow in the distance. I knew it was a woman because she had a distinct feminine shape, complete with a floor-length skirt. She stood there motionless.

I steadied my light on it and kept a hand on my pistol.

"Who's there?" I said. My voice sounded foreign in the tunnel, swallowed by the walls and thrown back into something low and strange.

NOTHING ANSWERED. I only heard a hollow drip and felt the faint rush of air. The figure still didn't move. When I got close enough, I could see she was wrapped head to toe in black. She was wearing a black veil long enough to brush the floor.

I blinked, incredulous. I adjusted the angle of my headlamp, but she remained. The black fabric swallowed the light without giving much back. The Widow of Whitcomb Hill. I even heard her sob.

For a heartbeat, I almost believed the story, especially because of the sobbing. I had nearly drawn my pistol until I realized the cry was the same, and it was playing in a loop.

Every pause between sobs was identical. The

pitch never wavered. Real grief has rhythm, and this was metronomic.

I let out a long breath and shook my head. Theatrics.

I stepped forward, light aimed straight at her face. I lifted her veil to nothing but a mannequin's head. The plaster of her cheeks chipped to reveal gray beneath. Her eyes were painted and glossy. She had a small, mischievous smile.

Whoever staged this had a flair for the dramatic and a keen sense of psychology. This Widow was placed here to trick anyone who wandered this far. Fear was a cheap deterrent. Clever.

I saw the little box at her side. It was a black speaker with a motion sensor. A cheap trick.

But effective, I had to admit. In the dark, the recording paired with a figure like that, even a rational mind might hesitate. I had, for just a second. And a second was all fear ever needed.

I crouched beside the speaker, my headlamp bouncing off the tunnel wall. The model was new, one of those battery-powered outdoor types sold at hardware stores. The dust hadn't settled evenly on the casing. Someone had been down here and fumbled with it within the past week.

If they had taken the trouble to set a fake Widow

here, deep in the tunnel, to deter anyone from going farther, it made me even more curious about what was hiding down here.

I let out a short laugh under my breath. Ghost legends certainly made convenient guards.

I switched off the wailing speaker with a flick of my glove. The sobs were annoying me. I would turn it back on on the way back.

Once I moved past the Widow, there was still only one path forward, so I knew I couldn't get lost. The ground sloped slightly downward. The walls widened by degrees, and I no longer needed to crouch. The air shifted from cold to cool, tinged with something metallic beneath the river scent. Machinery? Storage? I couldn't tell yet.

I walked for a while until I came to a crossroads of tunnels. I had three path options, but I didn't have to choose one because I saw two small crates sitting before one tunnel. Maybe there were more in other tunnels.

The crates I could see now were stacked one on top of the other. Modern bolts reinforced the seams, steel brackets biting into the wood. These weren't meant to be pried open with a crowbar. Whoever sealed them had planned for the long haul.

I brushed my gloved fingers across one lid. No

dust or cobwebs. Someone had brought them down here recently.

I angled my light toward the lower crate and found faint stenciled letters near the corner. The paint was smudged, but I could make it out: "C-V-R."

I didn't recognize it, but I took a guess that it was the destination code for where the crates were going.

Opening one of those crates would leave a trail I couldn't control. I didn't have to know what was inside. I just wanted to know who was responsible for them for now.

I stood there a long moment, listening for any sign of life. It was quiet here tonight.

I took out my tracker, which was no bigger than a nickel. I slid it into a narrow gap between the wood panels. It was wedged in tight enough that it was unlikely to be shaken loose even if the crate was hauled for miles.

And wherever these crates would travel to, I'd be following.

NINE

The tracker pinged just after midnight.

I was at my desk when the little blue dot on my phone app for the tracker blinked insistently to get my attention. The crates I had tagged were on the move. Adrenaline surged through me, sharpening everything. I needed to get going again. Whatever was happening beneath Cheerville wouldn't stay underground for long.

I slid the phone into my pocket and reached for my pistol. Age might have thinned my hair and stiffened my joints, but some things the body never forgot. One practiced motion and it was back in its holster at my side, the leather swallowing it without complaint. I checked the rest of my things in my bag, making sure I didn't need anything else. Preparedness cost nothing, while regret cost plenty.

As I passed Dandelion napping in a corner, I slipped outside and pulled the door closed. He flicked one ear but didn't bother opening his eyes.

"Guard the house," I whispered. His ears twitched again as if to say, *I always do*.

The night air was cold against my face. My car sat under the thin wash of moonlight. I slid into the driver's seat and pulled the phone out.

The insistent dot pulsated across the digital map of Cheerville. The crates were definitely moving.

They traced a slow path through town, cutting north before turning toward the river.

I drove until the tracker's pulse slowed near the water, then eased the car beneath the branches of a wide elm. Its shadow swallowed the vehicle whole. I cut the engine, let the silence settle, and slipped out, closing the door with the softest click.

My breath fogged once before dissolving. I touched my pistol to make sure it was secure, and then set my phone to its lowest brightness.

On foot was safer from here. I had a feeling where the crates were going.

The riverfront had always drawn the town's

quiet dealings. Cheerville didn't advertise its past, but the docks still bore the memory of Prohibition, when barrels rolled here under moonlight and disappeared into barges bound for other states.

Now the old warehouses leaned into the black water as if they were too tired to stand, their broken reflections twisting in the current. Pilings jutted from the river like rotten teeth. Gulls cried from somewhere inside the fog. The air smelled faintly of diesel, river silt, and old rope, a cocktail that had soaked into the timbers decades ago and never left. The docks were the kind of place you came only when duty forced you. No one visited them for pleasure.

I slowed my steps, rolling heel to toe to keep my footing silent. Every sense switched on: sight scanning for movement, hearing filtering for voices over the lap of the current, smell marking anything out of place.

Tonight one warehouse wasn't sleeping. A thin crease of yellow light spilled through the gap in its doors. Beneath it, the steady thump of a generator gave the building a mechanical heartbeat.

This was meant to be a fast job, in and out. Whoever set it up wasn't an amateur but wasn't worried about drawing attention either. That meant they didn't expect company. I smiled a little.

I slipped down behind a stack of discarded pallets and let my eyes adjust. Stillness was a spy's first ally. Give people long enough, and they'd reveal what they meant to hide. I pressed my cheek briefly against the rough wood, using its edge as a sightline. The light inside flickered with movement.

Soon, the doors eased open. A heavyset man I didn't recognize pulled out a dolly with two small crates. They looked like the ones from the tunnel. I recognized the second man as the bland man who had rolled out of the carriage house window.

He moved with the same easy balance. I had a feeling he could break a neck before anyone blinked.

The bland man went over to a small, run-down fishing boat. The other was tasked with loading the crates onto it. I could guess what was inside. Weapons, drugs, maybe dangerous tech. Whatever it was, it was valuable enough to kill for, and worth hiding under the town's feet until the time was right to move it.

Their movements were efficient. This wasn't their first run. When the job was done, the men started to relax and joke around. I could only catch part of their conversation.

"...close the Cheerville route... heat after the old lady's accident..."

My jaw clenched. Old lady. Were they talking about me?

Then the nondescript man murmured something I could barely catch.

"...Halloween...the last night... quiet after..."

"...one last run... a shame that... easy money..."

I leaned closer, careful not to shift the pallets. Their words carried in fragments, snatched between the generator's hum and the river's lap. But they had told me enough. Patrick's death and Tyler's accident were likely attracting too much attention for them to continue here.

They were pulling the plug on Cheerville, but they were going to pull one last run on Halloween, likely because the town and police would be distracted by the Ghost Walk.

That meant if I was going to catch them, I had to do it on Halloween night.

...after the old lady's accident...

Who else could they have meant? They might be onto me. Were they planning on going after me and making it seem like an accident? I couldn't imagine any other old lady who would be threatening to their cause, expect maybe if one of the Historical Society committee members knew too much.

If they wanted to make an example of me or anyone else, that meant they were the ones responsible for Tyler's accident, and likely Patrick's death.

As the boat left the dock with the bland man steering it, I'd seen enough. I slipped back to my car. I checked my phone. The tracker definitely showed the crates moving along the river. I could follow it, but that wasn't the point anymore. One shipment was gone, but more crates waited in the tunnels.

I stood for a moment by the driver's door, watching the faint light of the boat bob away into fog. Somewhere upriver, their buyers or business partners were waiting.

I had to be ready for Halloween. I slid the car into gear and let it roll. As I drove, I thought about my next steps.

If these men wanted to make Barbara Gold a ghost story, they were going to have to work for it. And I planned to be there when the lights came up and the curtain dropped.

Halloween wasn't just their opportunity anymore. It was mine. They thought they could use the town's biggest distraction to disappear. I'd turn that distraction into a trap.

By the time the clock struck midnight on Halloween, they were going to be immortalized into Cheerville's next legends.

As I sped up, I was smiling. I had the perfect plan. Liz would have her best role to date.

TEN

Cheerville never let anything ruin a holiday. Not blizzards, not power outages, and certainly not a dead antiques dealer. This was a town that prided itself on resilience, though some might call it stubbornness. Over the years, it had learned to fold disaster into the schedule and carry on with a smile.

Once, a tree had fallen onto a major street during the Christmas parade. The parade paused for six minutes, then resumed right around the fallen tree as if it were a fun detour. If catastrophe wanted attention, it had to buy a ticket.

Patrick Halloway's sudden demise was tragic, yes, but it had also become the kind of publicity the Historical Society couldn't have paid for if they tried. Naturally, they tried to keep it quiet. Or pretended to. The official statements were careful: "tragic accident," "unexpected loss," "nothing to fear." It was almost admirable how quickly they pivoted from condolences to ticket sales.

But Cheerville was a sieve for gossip. By the time the local paper printed its sanitized headline, half the town already had its own version of the story. In one, Patrick had been poisoned by a jealous rival dealer. In another, he'd found cursed jewelry. My favorite was the one where the Widow herself had dragged him to the underworld for staging tacky decorations. Word slipped across backyard fences and into text chains faster than any press release, compounding into folklore.

The flyers promised a Ghost Walk "bigger and better than ever," and the town rose to meet the claim. Cheerville dressed for the occasion like it was auditioning for a movie set. Storefronts sagged under fake cobwebs. Skeletons grinned from second-floor windows. Jack-o'-lanterns glowed in rows along the old stone church steps. The air smelled like caramel, woodsmoke, and sugar, enough to make your teeth ache just walking through it. Fog machines pumped steady clouds across the sidewalks, blurring the edges of everything. Somewhere above, a speaker blasted eerie music that looped every thirty seconds. People seemed to love it.

Children ran ahead of their parents, plastic pumpkin buckets clacking against their knees. Teenagers elbowed each other into shrieks, laughing too loud and ducking into alleyways with their phones lit. Couples walked arm in arm, clutching cider and hot cocoa and pretending not to flinch when a volunteer ghost jumped from a doorway.

Vendors sold "Widow's Tears" lemonade and "Smuggler's Fudge." Someone had even parked a food truck selling mini cakes in the shapes of coffins.

The screams were half real, half rehearsed. The laughter rolled down Main Street in waves. Tourism was booming. People had come in from two or three towns over just to gawk at our brush with mystery. Patrick's death had worked its way into the evening, a subplot whispered about in lineups and exaggerated for dramatic effect.

I heard the phrase "the murder house" used to describe the carriage house. It had become a landmark before the coroner's report was even finished. I wondered if they'd add it back to next year's Ghost Walk.

My grandson Martin was out there somewhere, enjoying the evening like every other kid with a sweet tooth and a smartphone. I didn't need to spot him to know he was grinning, probably filming something for Instagram while juggling a fistful of candy. He was getting older now, but I wanted him to keep his innocence for as long as he could. If I couldn't see him tonight, I'd have to check his social media to see exactly what he got up to.

Above ground, the night was all sugar and spooky spectacle. Below, I was heading for a place where men didn't hesitate to turn other men into ghosts.

While the rest of Cheerville was playing dress-up, I was dressed in black from collar to shoes, a custom that did double duty. I passed as one more grandmother, just another tired woman shuffling through the crowd. To anyone glancing my way, I looked like someone heading home to hand out candy. Nothing in my gait or expression said I was planning to slip below the town and bait a smuggling syndicate under cover of carnival noise.

The carriage house stood apart from it all, a condemned footnote, closed off and forgotten. The police had done their part to make it look off-limits. Grimal's officers had wrapped a thick new chain across the front door after someone spotted teenagers poking around the property. The signage, printed in bold red letters, warned of structural instability.

The crowd flowed past the carriage house without a second glance, funneled by the Historical Society's rope barriers and signs pointing toward cheerier stops. They had jack-o'-lanterns, string lights, and costumed volunteers waiting up ahead. No one lingered near the carriage house. Even the fake fog seemed to avoid this stretch, rolling past in long ribbons. The noise and laughter thinned around it, leaving a stillness in its wake.

And that was exactly what we needed. Liz stood at the edge of the lot, half in shadow, her black backpack slung over one shoulder. When she spotted me, she gave a short nod and fell into step.

She had tied her hair back, tucked under a knit cap. She'd listened to my briefing and followed all the steps. Her outfit was regulation practical: black pants, dark jacket, nothing shiny. She's skipped the perfume and even scented shampoos. Any fragrance would've been too traceable.

We moved along the fringe, letting the music and chatter mask our pace. Once we slipped beyond the last pool of lantern light, we stood still.

From where we stood, the carriage house looked like something holding its breath.

The front door was out of the question, but the side window was just as I remembered it.

Liz looked it over. "Window?"

"Window," I said.

And we got to work.

I stepped forward first, testing the frame with my fingers. With a little pressure and patience, the board gave way with a low groan that sounded barely audible against the hum of distant laughter. I paused, listening, but I heard nothing from within the carriage house. I pulled the panel higher.

"After you?" Liz murmured.

I swung one leg over and eased myself through. My boots met the floor with a muted thud. I straightened and scanned the room before nodding her in. Liz climbed after me with her usual economy of motion.

We didn't speak once we were inside. I watched Liz take in the décor still where it had been staged the night Patrick's body tumbled out. The Widow hunched forever over her coffin, her veil graying more with dust. The shackled skeleton slumped against the wall in permanent defeat. Even knowing the truth, I felt a shiver crawl up the back of my neck.

"We do this fast," Liz said.

"Fast and clean," I said.

She unzipped her backpack and gave me a gas mask, while she put on the rest of her costume. The mask was cold in my hands. The faint chemical smell brought back memories I hadn't planned on revisiting, being in rooms where the air could kill you faster than a bullet. I didn't need to put it on yet, and I hung it around my neck.

We crossed to the center of the room. I crouched, running my gloved fingers along the floorboards until they found the false panel. The wood creaked softly. I lifted the panel and set it aside.

Liz leaned in behind me. "That's cool," she muttered as she stared at the trapdoor. "I can't believe it's been here the whole time."

"This town certainly keeps getting more interesting," I agreed.

When I pulled the door open, she stared at the dark gap. "Whoa."

There was nothing for Liz to assess, so she simply had to follow me down the ladder.

She gave a short, humorless breath. "Figures," she said. "You always pick the scenic routes."

I turned on my headlamp. I felt for the edge of the ladder with my boot and gave it a small test. The iron rung held.

"You ready?" I asked.

Liz nodded once. "Let's go."

I went first. The cold deepened with each rung. Liz followed close behind. The sound of the crowd's laughter and shouts faded above us. The trapdoor above stayed open, but the glow didn't reach far. Once we were in the tunnels, the dark closed in again.

Every movement echoed too loudly no matter how quiet we tried to be going down the ladder. The tunnels were even colder than I remembered. The temperature had dropped in the past few days, but it made a vast difference down here. The cold seemed to rise from the bottom, nipping at my ankles, then the knees, wrapping around my spine.

My breath fogged, curling up into the beam of my light. Liz muttered something about "Cheerville's underworld air-conditioning," but her voice was tight. She felt it too, the biting cold that came from stone, not weather.

My headlamp beam cut forward in a tight line. The tunnel curved ahead as it had the last time.

I slowed when I saw the fake Widow, heard the fake cries from the little speaker. I could hear Liz behind me stifling a snort of laughter.

"Ten out of ten for commitment," she whispered. "Creepy *and* low budget."

We pushed past the Widow, though Liz curtseyed as she passed out of respect.

We kept walking for some time until I stepped to the intersection of tunnels where I had found the two crates last time. Of course, those crates were long gone now.

I snapped off my headlamp. Immediately, I saw that one of the tunnels had a faint glow. I gestured for Liz to follow me into that tunnel.

The air smelled of sharply of metallic machinery. The glow ahead flickered weakly. I figured it was from a single lantern.

As I got closer, I was right. I saw that the glow came from a battery lantern. It cast long shadows against the stone. I heard men's voices. They were speaking as if they didn't have a reason to whisper.

"Last load... But plenty of work still in Greenville."

The second voice had a grin tucked inside it. "Too bad...Easiest job I've had..."

"Don't worry.... We'll come back as soon as things settle down...."

Liz's hand touched my arm lightly to give a signal.

We were both counting the voices. Two, so far. The light shifted again, showing their outlines moving around stacked crates. They were unloading fast.

They were too comfortable down here. They believed they were alone. They were wrong.

Being comfortable dulled the senses. It made people sloppy. I had seen better-trained men than these lose everything because they mistook routine for safety.

From the edge of the glow, I watched. Three of them in total, the third one being the bland man who almost caught me by the alley dumpster. They were busy loading more crates onto a dolly, moving like men who had done this too many times to bother thinking about it. Their eyes stayed fixed on the crate in front of them, not once glancing toward the open mouth of the passage where we loitered. The labor took their focus, leaving their breathing shallow. The smell of oil and sweat hung thick.

I cataloged them automatically. One heavyset, favoring his left knee, would be slower in a chase. One lean and less confident, a follower. And the bland man, efficient, precise, the leader.

I counted their motions, the rhythm of their effort, the pause before the next heave. I waited until

I could slip my own movements into the gaps. I pulled the gas mask on.

The rubber sealed against my face with a muffled pop. My breath echoed faintly inside the filter, the sound too close to my ears. Every inhale made the world seem smaller. I didn't mind it. Smaller meant focus.

Then I began to move as silently as I could. The heavyset man let out a grunt as he wrestled the dolly forward, his partner steadying the crate strapped above with both hands. The bland man was ahead on the other side. Timing had always been my ally, and I had found my window.

I darted forward, keeping low. My hand closed around the electric lantern. With one controlled swing, I smashed it against the far wall.

It shattered with a pop and hiss, sparks flashing out like fireflies before dying in the dark. Glass burst into sharp pieces. The tunnel dropped into sudden, total darkness.

Before they even spoke, I could feel their confusion fill the space.

"Hey!" the lean man shouted, his voice cracking against the stone.

I pressed myself against the wall and slid along it, invisible now that the light was gone.

"Who's there?" the heavyset man demanded. His voice was sharp, with a thin edge of unease.

I gave him silence.

They cursed, fumbling for their phones. I could hear the scuffle of boots, the sharp slap of palms searching pockets. In their panic, one of them dropped something, likely the phone they had managed to pull out.

It was Liz's turn to shine now.

We didn't need to do the next part, but it was Halloween, after all. Everyone else in town was having fun tonight. Why couldn't we?

Liz waited for one of the men to get their act together and turn on a light source. Then it was time to make her grand entrance.

ELEVEN

The men reacted immediately. They panicked, still fumbling around in the dark. They were taking too long. Liz and I became impatient. Each movement was jerky and louder than the last. Fear always made people louder. They cursed, boots scraping against stone, one of them knocking into the dolly with a metallic clatter that echoed far too loud in the enclosed space.

The heavyset man finally got his phone out, hands shaking when the flashlight finally came on. The narrow beam quivered as it slid down the wall and landed on Liz.

Liz moved slowly. She stepped into the edge of the glow like an apparition made real. The black veil swallowed her face completely. The lean man made a noise halfway between a curse and a prayer. The legend they'd disregarded as a joke had come walking toward them in flesh and bone.

Then came the sound. It began as a soft, shuddering sob, then another, stretched out until it echoed down the tunnel. Liz had mastered the cries of mourning. It was uncanny, not just because it sounded real, but because it seemed to echo as though grief had taken up residence in the stone.

It raised goosebumps. Even I felt a fear crawl along my skin, and I knew Liz was the one making the sounds.

Liz was enjoying this role a little too much. The cries rose and fell, bouncing off the walls in faint, distorted fragments. She was doing a fantastic job as the Widow reborn.

The men only stared, mouths agape.

Her hands pressed together in a prayer position. Her veil swayed slightly with each deliberate step, the fabric catching the flashlight beam. If the sight of her wasn't so terrifying, I would've called this pure artistry, through and through.

"Jesus," the heavyset man said under his breath.

The phone wobbled, almost slipping from his hand. Liz stepped forward again with glacial slowness.

The two smugglers swore aloud, bumping into the dolly and then each other. The crates on top rocked dangerously.

"Don't be stupid," the bland man snapped. "This is a trick. It's just a joke."

His voice was sharp and angry, though it wavered near the end. He was trying to command the room again, but belief had already shifted.

But the other two weren't listening. They had gone pale. The Widow had taken the lead. The one with the phone took another step back, the beam bouncing wildly. His chest was heaving, breath sharp and shallow. "She moved," he said. "She moved!"

"Keep it together," the bland man barked. "It's just some volunteer who wandered down here."

"She's real," the lean man said. "It's her. It's the Widow!"

For a moment, I could almost feel the old legend slithering through the tunnel with us. The men's belief had made it real. Once fear joined the story, it didn't matter what was true. Fear was enough to make ghosts out of the living.

In the shadows behind the crates, I steadied my breath and reached for the canister at my belt. The straps of the gas mask were already tight across my face. Liz already had hers on beneath the veil.

I twisted the valve. The canister gave a sharp hiss. The sound filled the tunnel, curling through the cold air.

The men froze again, confusion flickering across their faces. They looked at one another, unsure of what to do.

The first cough came a beat later. Then another. The air thickened quickly, carrying the fine mist through the confined space.

"What the hell—"

The words broke into hacking. The phone beam wobbled, dropped, and landed faceup on the ground. It did even spookier things to Liz's image. For a second, she looked like she was made of smoke. The light bounced against the stone ceiling, creating a trembling pool of white.

Liz didn't move. She stood still at the center, a black silhouette surrounded by fog, her breathing slow and steady under the mask. Her soft, broken sobbing continued. I had to hand it to her. She had a second career as a horror theatre actress. The fog curled around her skirts. Her shadow stretched across the floor, ghostly in the quivering light.

Her performance was wasted now that the smugglers coughed harder. One doubled over. The second clawed at his shirt, stumbling into the dolly. The smell of the gas was faint but acrid, enough to sting the back of the throat even from where I crouched. It blurred the mind, slowed the body, and turned strong men into staggering shapes. I'd used it before, years ago, in basements a long way from Cheerville. Funny how these skills still had their uses in retirement.

Soon, the smugglers' bodies collapsed, one after another. They hit the ground with heavy, uncoordinated thuds. The crates rocked again but stayed upright.

The last to fall was the bland man. He was strong. If he hadn't been a criminal, he would've made a good recruit. He braced against the wall, staring into the haze where Liz still stood. For a brief moment, he looked at her like he could still force an explanation into existence. Then he crumpled.

The tunnel went still after the faint hiss of the gas stopped. The smoke thinned in uneven curls, revealing what we'd made of the scene: men down, crates stacked, a ghost standing guard.

"Time," I said. My voice was muffled inside the mask, but Liz heard it.

She turned on her flashlight. The light revealed more clearly the bodies slumped against the wall.

"Efficient," she murmured. Her tone carried the

satisfaction of a woman who had just rebalanced the universe.

We moved fast. I pulled zip ties from a pocket and bound wrists tightly together while Liz pulled out rope from her bag, and started tying them up. I double-checked every tie.

When the last body was secured with rope, I took a step back, scanning our work. The men would wake up groggy, disoriented, and gift-wrapped for Grimal's team. He'd get the credit, but we weren't doing this for the glory.

We hurried back through the tunnel from where we came, passing the other fake Widow, then up the ladder. I continued to hear Liz doing her Widow wail. She couldn't seem to resist squeezing a few more shivers out of the night. Somewhere behind us, the tunnel carried the sound.

By the time we reached the trapdoor, it was hard to tell which echo belonged to her and which the tunnel had decided to keep.

Up in the carriage house we removed our masks. With the veil thrown to the side, I saw Liz's face flushed with sweat and triumph. The adrenaline hadn't worn off. She grinned widely.

"You really enjoyed playing the Widow," I said.

She wiped her forehead with her sleeve. "What about you? Stealing my thunder with the crying."

"What do you mean?"

"You were good. Creepy, even."

"I didn't do anything."

"Yes you did. With all the sobbing and wailing."

I blinked. "That wasn't me."

Liz frowned. "Then who—"

"I thought it was you."

She shook her head. "Couldn't have been. The mask muffled everything."

"Same here," I said. "It would have sounded wrong."

We looked at each other for a moment, both of us trying to fit reason into what we'd heard. The tunnel below yawned open at our feet. Its black mouth seemed to mock us.

I thought about the fake Widow mannequin near the tunnel entrance. Maybe the speaker had been left running, but it had been too far away. The cries we heard had been close enough to be next to our ears.

I tried to blame the echo, the air pressure, the distortion of sound through stone. None of it made sense.

"You're joking," Liz said quietly.

"No," I answered. "It wasn't me, I swear."

A small shiver slid down my spine. I went through all the logical reasons again and came up with nothing. The hair along my neck had risen before I even realized it.

Then, deciding to focus on the practical, I reached into my pocket for my phone. The disguiser app was already open.

I pressed the button, tested the sound which flattened and distorted my voice.

"Come to the carriage house. There's a trap door that goes down to the tunnels. Three smugglers are down there, tied up. Send your chief."

Before the operator could respond, I ended the call. Taking questions only slowed down the cavalry.

That was when I heard it. A laugh. High, thin, and unmistakably female. It seemed to come from within the tunnel. We stared down into the darkness.

I turned to Liz. Her eyes were wide.

"Was that—" I started.

Her hand came up sharply. "Not me."

The laugh returned, fainter now, drifting backward into the dark until it was little more than an echo. It lingered for a breath, then disappeared completely.

TWELVE

By the time the police went down into the tunnels, most of Cheerville was already in front of the carriage house. People huddled close, breath puffing in clouds. The blue and red strobes of police cars bounced off costumes, turning the Halloween night into a spectacle.

Tourists leaned forward with eager eyes, ready to capture whatever they could for their feeds and stories to tell back home. The locals packed in tighter, each one convinced they had some right to be there, as if proximity might grant them ownership of the tale. Snippets of speculation floated through the air: "I heard they found a whole armory." "No, no, it's drugs, obviously." "My dad said there was a ghost down there."

"Back up, folks," an officer barked. His voice strained against the noise. "Clear some room. Back up."

Naturally, not a single person moved. Cheerville had perfected the art of rubbernecking. Elderly women in quilted coats nudged each other like they were vying for a prime spot at a church bake sale. Teenagers ducked and slipped through gaps, phones held high. Some were already narrating for their followers, their voices full of breathless drama. The men at the edge of the lawn stood with hands in their pockets, shoulders squared, pretending they were part of the response team instead of gawking spectators.

I stayed on the outskirts at first, keeping my head down. Crowds like this were perfect to disappear into.

Liz had already slipped away earlier, claiming she wanted to give out Halloween candy to trick-or-treaters with her husband. I suspected she didn't want him to worry, or didn't want to explain where she'd disappeared off to for so long. Either way, she'd earned her exit.

I stayed. After everything, it felt right to see how the night ended. If I was honest, I wanted a bit of a show too. I also wanted to make sure Grimal's men managed to do their jobs. Part of me, the old operative part, needed to see the operation fully handed off before I allowed myself to exhale. Would they be too scared by the fake Widow guarding the tunnel entrance to find the smugglers?

Knowing how Grimal reacted to the mannequin Widow in the carriage house, I'd have loved to have been down there in the tunnels to see whether or not he'd bolt at the sight of the fake Widow and sound machine.

I looked for Octavian, but he didn't seem to be around. Maybe he was at the Historical Society, giving the end of one tour. He'd said he'd been instructed to sell the history of the Historical Society building for "authentic atmosphere." I smiled faintly at the thought. He had no idea how authentic things had just become here.

But I spotted my grandson ahead of me in the crowd. Martin had shot up taller since summer. I'd recognize the back of his head anywhere. He held his phone above the sea of heads like a periscope, filming the scene below with the seriousness of a documentarian. Beside him, my son stood with arms folded. Neither of them noticed me a few paces back. I thought about catching up to them, but the fatigue pressed into my bones. I was too exhausted to play the aghast grandmother tonight.

Martin's voice carried faintly above the crowd. "Did they find the secret tunnels?"

His father didn't respond, but a man nearby said it was more likely some teenagers who broke in to get drunk.

As cold and damp as the night was, the body heat of the crowd made me too hot. Still, I wanted to stay until they brought the men out. I wouldn't even mind Grimal boasting he masterminded finding the tunnels himself as long as he wrapped this up quick.

After another hour, the first two smugglers appeared, hauled up from the tunnels by the officers. Their wrists were bound, eyes squinting under the harsh lights. They stumbled in the men's grip, stripped of any bravado they had belowground. Their boots left wet tracks across the grass. The flash from someone's phone camera caught the heavyset man mid-blink, freezing him forever in that moment of defeat.

The jeering crowd quieted to take a better look. The smugglers looked less like dangerous men and more like damp rats dragged into the open. The crowd gasped collectively, leaning closer as if they might read guilt from the lines on each man's face. A few mothers drew their children back by the sleeves, though none of them actually left.

Then came the last man, the blandest one. His plain jacket hung off one shoulder. His face was expressionless, though his eyes stayed sharp. They moved over the crowd, and then they found me. The yard narrowed down to just him and me. The look was brief, no more than a second, but it was recognition, clear and cold. His gaze only broke when the officers shoved him toward the waiting van. I understood the message perfectly: this wasn't over.

He had not been surprised to see me. I would bet that I was that old lady he had planned to put in an accident.

Chief Grimal strutted out into the scene like a man stepping onto a stage. His chest was puffed out, his belt hitched high.

"Smuggling operation," he announced to the reporters gathered at the gate. "Significant one. You'll get more details once the evidence is processed." His voice carried across the yard, loud enough for the crowd to repeat it before he had even finished. Microphones leaned in. Cameras flashed. Grimal soaked it all in.

Reporters asked if the tunnels were real.

Grimal nodded once, tried to look humble, but projected the voice again. "I can confirm the tunnels are real."

The crowd broke out in loud chatter.

I caught a familiar voice in front of me. "Unbelievable," Martin said to his dad. "I knew it! I knew the tunnels had to be real!"

The officers slammed the van doors shut with a heavy thud. The sound folded into the crowd and set people talking again.

Rumors began to thread through the noise like a new kind of decoration. A young man started livestreaming, narrating in a breathless voice everything that had happened so far.

I was about to turn away when I noticed Gerald Whitlow standing near the lamppost at the edge of the crowd. His posture was too still for the chaos around him. He wasn't craning for a better look like everyone else. He was watching the van with a faint frown, his gaze following it until the taillights disappeared down the road. There was calculation in the set of his jaw.

I studied him for another moment before I turned and walked away for good. The night had given the town a story. While the tunnels were a big discovery, and the smugglers were likely responsible for Patrick's death, the case hadn't wrapped up as neatly as I would've liked, but it had given me more leads. Tonight, I was beat, but I intended to follow them on another day.

I couldn't prove it yet, but I had a feeling Gerald Whitlow played a part in the smuggling ring. He was someone I would be keeping a close eye on.

———

OCTAVIAN SAT at my kitchen table the next morning, the newspapers spread wide across the wood like he owned a news stand. His coffee had gone cold beside him, forgotten in favor of the headlines.

The front page screamed in bold type: **_SMUGGLERS EXPOSED BENEATH CHEERVILLE! SECRET TUNNELS CONFIRMED!_** Fonts so large they could have knocked over furniture. A grainy photo of the carriage house filled the center. The papers had milked every inch of drama from it.

Every few seconds came a hum of amusement or a short laugh under his breath. Then he barked out a full laugh. He showed me one page where the Widow figure had been Photoshopped onto a photo of the carriage house, complete with fog and a superimposed question mark.

"Well, I'll be damned," he said, slapping the paper with the flat of his hand. "The stories get better and better."

I sipped my tea and said nothing.

"And right under our noses too, the tunnels," he continued. "Five towns, maybe more. They say this Nigel fellow ran the whole thing like clockwork. I wonder how much loot he moved."

"It must've been worth millions for him to go through the trouble," I said.

"Patrick had discovered they were using his shipments to move their shady wares, and they offed him. Poor guy."

"And Tyler? The same guys were onto him and tried to send a message, right?"

"That's what it says." Octavian flicked the paper.

"I want to know who discovered the tunnels in the first place," I said. "These guys couldn't have been smart enough."

He leaned back, still grinning. "Time will reveal all. But this part—this part is the best. The paper says it was *her*."

"Her?" I asked.

"The Widow," he said, delighted. "The Widow of Whitcomb Hill herself. According to the article, she's the one who scared the smugglers witless and tipped off the police. She was the one who got justice for Patrick and found his murderers."

He waited for me to laugh. I didn't.

"Maybe they're right," I said mildly.

He chuckled, shaking his head. "You're teasing me."

"This theory is actually in the paper?" I asked.

Octavian laughed again, passing the paper to me. "And you think journalism is dead."

"If it wasn't the Widow, who could it be?" I asked, half-joking, half-serious.

"Well, whoever it was, they saved this town from turning into someone else's storage unit. That's worth a toast."

He raised his mug, and I met it with mine.

Earlier, Octavian had told me that Tyler had woken up last night and was already complaining about how bad the hospital food was. By the sound of it, he'd be back to lecturing anyone who would listen by the end of the week.

"That boy will be insufferable soon," Octavian

said, smiling. "He'll memorize every article in the paper and start correcting the journalists."

"He's earned the right to brag," I said. "He was right about the tunnels."

Octavian gave me a look over the top of the paper. He took another sip of coffee. "Still, I can't believe anyone in this town truly thinks the Widow had anything to do with it. That's just the paper trying to sell copies, isn't it?"

I ran a finger around the rim of my cup. "Ghosts are tidy explanations."

"Tidy," he repeated.

He studied me for a moment, then tilted his head, expecting me to continue.

I didn't at first. What could I tell him? That I had heard sobbing in those tunnels long after the gas had settled? That a woman's laugh followed us out?

"Maybe it was the Widow," I murmured, mostly to myself.

Octavian's brow lifted. "Barbara Gold, do you believe in ghosts now?"

I looked him straight in the eye. "Anything's possible, dear."

He laughed softly, and leaned in to kiss me on my head. He stood up to refill his coffee. My eyes caught the page from the newspaper. The Widow stared back at me from the illustration, her veil trailing like smoke, her painted hands reaching toward me.

For a moment, I thought I heard something that sounded like a sob coming from the living room.

I flicked my head to the sound, but it was only Dandelion, striding in with a toy mouse in his mouth.

ABOUT THE AUTHOR

Harper Lin is a *USA TODAY* bestselling cozy mystery author. When she's not reading or writing mysteries, she loves going to yoga classes, hiking, and baking with her family and friends.

For a complete list of her books by series, visit her website.

www.HarperLin.com